PRAISE FOR THE NATIONAL BESTSELLING
RAVEN'S NEST BOOKSTORE MYSTERIES

Trouble Vision

"Allison Kingsley . . . has written another enjoyable mystery with very likable characters and a light, humorous tone sure to please." —*Kings River Life*

"Kingsley's use of the paranormal in this series is exceptional." —*Debbie's Book Bag*

A Sinister Sense

"The second Raven's Nest Bookstore mystery throws Clara's love interest, Rick Sanders, right in the middle of a murder. Clara's personal interest in solving the crime adds to the plausibility of her actions, and characters and relationships are further fleshed out in this novel." —*RT Book Reviews*

"An entertaining, amusing whodunit as the two cousins who are BFF 'sisters' land in one mess after another . . . Fans will enjoy this lighthearted, well-written mystery."
—*Genre Go Round Reviews*

Mind Over Murder

"A delightful read . . . [A] winning addition to the cozy paranormal mystery realm."
—Yasmine Galenorn, *New York Times* bestselling author

continued . . .

"The breakout must-read mystery of the fall season. [It] is a definite contender for best new cozy series of 2011 . . . Kingsley's inhabitants are a sensational cast of players with exhilarating and quirky personalities that vibrantly jump off the page, engaging the reader immediately."

—*Seattle Post-Intelligencer*

"A fun paranormal amateur sleuth . . . The story line is fast-paced throughout, regardless of whether the plot focuses on the whodunit or the men wanting to date lofty Clara. It is a sure bet that fans will want to return to the Raven's Nest bookstore for more Quinn Sense sensational stories."

—*Genre Go Round Reviews*

"Fast-paced and a quick read. This is a puzzling cozy that will appeal to a wide audience."   —*Once Upon a Romance*

"This series debut features a young psychic, a unique bookstore, and the charm of small-town Maine. The action starts early and the momentum builds through this cleverly plotted cozy . . . A good start to a promising new series."

—*RT Book Reviews*

Berkley Prime Crime titles by Allison Kingsley

MIND OVER MURDER
A SINISTER SENSE
TROUBLE VISION
EXTRA SENSORY DECEPTION

Extra Sensory Deception

Allison Kingsley

BERKLEY PRIME CRIME, NEW YORK

THE BERKLEY PUBLISHING GROUP
Published by the Penguin Group
Penguin Group (USA) LLC
375 Hudson Street, New York, New York 10014

USA • Canada • UK • Ireland • Australia • New Zealand • India • South Africa • China

penguin.com

A Penguin Random House Company

EXTRA SENSORY DECEPTION

A Berkley Prime Crime Book / published by arrangement with the author

For information, address: The Berkley Publishing Group,
a division of Penguin Group (USA) LLC,
375 Hudson Street, New York, New York 10014.

ISBN: 978-0-425-27138-4

PUBLISHING HISTORY
Berkley Prime Crime mass-market edition / August 2014

PRINTED IN THE UNITED STATES OF AMERICA

10 9 8 7 6 5 4 3 2 1

Cover illustration by Griesbach/Martucci. Cover design by George Long.
Interior text design by Laura K. Corless.

To my husband, for watching over me.

Acknowledgments

Many thanks to my editor, Michelle Vega, for caring about my characters as much as I do. Your help has been invaluable, and I'm grateful.

Thanks to my agent, Paige Wheeler, for all the great advice, support and encouragement—sometimes badly needed. You always come through.

To my very dear friends, Sam and Alan Willey, for your broad shoulders and willing ears. You made the coast of Maine come alive for me, and I thank you.

To Mr. Bill, who is always looking over my shoulder. Your pithy comments make my day.

To my fans, for your kind e-mails and posts. They mean so much to me, and I cherish every one.

1

The second Clara Quinn pushed open the door of the Raven's Nest bookstore, she knew she'd picked the wrong moment. For one thing, her cousin, Stephanie, stood behind the counter, holding a feather duster and wearing a red spot that burned in each cheek, which meant the infamous Quinn temper was in full bloom.

For another thing, the elegant blonde at the receiving end of Stephanie's fierce scowl was the owner of the stationer's next door, and a constant thorn in the sides of both cousins. Roberta Prince's fists dug into her slender hips and her voice was shrill with indignation as she demanded, "What do you mean—*bulldozed*? Are you suggesting I browbeat my customers into buying my products?"

Luckily Stephanie's full attention was on her opponent and she didn't see Clara gently close the door and back away from the store.

This was Tuesday, Clara's day off, and normally she would be relaxing on the beach in the warm May sunshine, watching Tatters chase the waves back into the sea. The big shaggy dog loved the water, and tirelessly bounded in and out until she called to him. Right now she'd give anything to be back on that beach, instead of facing the prospect of walking into a volcanic argument between her cousin and Roberta Prince.

Across the narrow street, a hunky dark-haired man balanced on a ladder while he pounded a nail into the nameboard of his hardware store.

For as long as Clara could remember, Parson's Hardware had been an institution in Finn's Harbor. Her father had practically used it as a second home, and every Saturday morning had stopped by, whether to buy the latest tools and gadgets or just to chat with Vern Parson. Now Vern was retired and her father had passed away, though the hardware store continued to thrive on Main Street.

Clara squinted against the sunlight as she watched the new owner fasten his own name above the door. She'd been dating Rick Sanders for a few weeks now, and was beginning to get used to the rush of pleasure she felt every time she saw him.

At first she'd been wary of getting involved again since her last disastrous relationship, but Rick had won her over with his thoughtfulness, honesty and fun-loving nature. She was gradually taking down the walls, and each time they were together she became a little more comfortable around him.

Smiling, she sauntered across the street, happy for the excuse to put off her visit to the bookstore.

Rick stared down at her when she called out to him, his gray eyes looking almost colorless in the glare reflected off the windows. "What are you doing in this neck of the woods? I thought this was your day off." He frowned at the nameboard, then, apparently satisfied, tucked his hammer into his tool belt and started down the ladder.

"It is. I'm running an errand for my mother."

"Glutton for punishment, huh?" Reaching the ground, he grinned at her. "Or is this just an excuse to come and see me?"

Clara laughed. "Maybe a little of both." She looked up at the nameboard. "Rick's Hardware. It has a nice ring to it."

"Yeah." He followed her gaze. "I've been meaning to change the name ever since I first bought the place. I thought about naming it Sanders's Hardware, but I think Rick sounds more appealing."

"Me, too." She sent a reluctant glance at the Raven's Nest. "I guess I'd better get over there and rescue Stephanie. She didn't look too happy just now."

"Roberta doing a number on her again?"

"Well, you know Roberta."

"Indeed I do." He took hold of the ladder, twisting his head to look at her over his shoulder. "Do you have a minute? I've got a favor to ask."

"Sure." She followed him into the store, waving to Tyler, his young assistant, as they walked by the check stand. Passing by shelves loaded with cans of paint, electrical supplies, an assortment of faucets, shower heads and bathroom cabinets, she wondered what kind of favor she'd agreed to do.

Rick stacked the ladder in the storeroom at the back of the store, and when he came out again, he held a roll of paper. "I promised a pal of mine I'd put one of these up in my window. He gave me a few of them, so I thought you might put one up in the bookstore."

She took the poster from him and unrolled it. "Oh, I heard about this—the Hometown Rodeo. It's part of the Memorial Day weekend festival."

"Yeah. The owners of the Hill Top Resort sponsored it. They thought it would add to the festival, now that their new resort has put Finn's Harbor on the map."

"It'll be different, that's for sure. I don't think there's ever been a rodeo around here, at least as long as I can remember."

"It should be fun." Rick tapped the poster with his forefinger. "My buddy, Wes Carlton, is a calf roper competing in it, so I said I'd help out by putting up the posters."

"Well, we'll be happy to help, too." Clara rolled up the poster. "We can put it next to the festival ad. I think—"

An anxious male voice from the other end of the store interrupted her. "Rick? Can you come here a minute?"

Rick frowned. "Sounds like Tyler's got something he can't handle."

He started up the aisle, and, abandoning what she was going to say, she followed him, calling out as she reached the door, "See you later."

Rick waved a hand in response, his attention on a customer who was curling his fingers around an imaginary object while he tried to explain what he wanted.

The sun warmed Clara's back as she waited at the curb for a line of cars to pass by. The sea breeze, heavy with the fragrance of sand and seaweed, fanned her face. On either side of Main Street, tourists strolled down the sidewalks, stopping every now and then to peer into the windows of the little shops.

Colorful awnings shaded them from the sun while they gazed at seashells and sand dollars, antique dolls and handcrafted jewelry, toy boats and rows of postcards depicting the Maine coast.

It hadn't been that long since Clara had left New York to return to her hometown, but already the memories of the bustling city were slipping away. At times like these, watching the sun sparkling on the water in the harbor at the base of the hill, she felt almost as if she'd never left

Finn's Harbor, and that her life in New York had been nothing more than a dream.

With a start she realized the road was clear, and darted across to the other side. Roberta was still standing at the counter when Clara pushed open the door. Stephanie, however, seemed calmer. Apparently the two women had settled their differences.

Her cousin looked surprised as Clara walked up to the counter. "You're supposed to be off today. What are you doing here?" Stephanie demanded, while Roberta ran her gaze up and down Clara as if she were examining an offensive statue.

Clara played a mental image of herself—jeans, sneakers, tank top and green striped shirt. Her dark hair had been blown around by the stiff sea breezes and she'd been putting off a haircut for way too long.

Roberta's slim black skirt was a tad too high above the knee. Her sandals added to her height by at least three inches. The crisp pink blouse bared her arms from the shoulder, and a string of pearls gleamed around her neck. She wore her smooth bleached hair pulled back in a bun and, unlike Clara, who had dashed a spot of lipstick across her mouth and dabbed at her eyelashes with the mascara brush, had obviously spent a good few minutes creating a masterpiece on her face.

Suppressing a sigh, Clara turned to her cousin. "I need to buy a copy of *Flight to Marcana*. Mom can't find it in the library and she's dying to read it. I promised her I'd pick up a copy for her today."

Stephanie nodded at the closest aisle. "It's a great book. There's some on the end display."

"I'll get one." Clara walked over to the end display, automatically patting the shoulder of Madam Sophia, the lifesize model of a fortune-teller that served as one of the store's mascots, before plucking a copy of the book from the shelf.

"I'll never understand why people read that garbage," Roberta said, as Clara carried the book back to the counter. "All that crap about other worlds in outer space. Vampires and ghosts, people traveling through time—no wonder our children are growing up with identity problems. They don't know how to deal with the real world."

Stephanie looked as if her hackles were rising again. Clara laid the book on the counter, saying mildly, "Fantasy and sci-fi books are extremely popular, which is why we specialize in them and why the Raven's Nest does so well. *Normal* people know it's fiction. They don't take it literally."

Apparently offended by the insinuation that she wasn't normal, Roberta gave her a lethal look. "Well, maybe they should. There's too much violence in those things. It's bound to have an effect on children's minds."

They'd had the same argument before, and knowing Roberta, there was no point in continuing it with her now.

Wisely, Clara decided to change the subject instead. She held up the poster to show it to her cousin. "I told Rick we'd put this up in the window."

Stephanie took it from her. "What is it?"

"A poster for the rodeo. Remember, Tim told us about it the other day?"

Roberta sniffed. "Tim Rossi seems to spend an awful lot of time in here for a deputy sheriff. You'd think he'd have better things to do, like chasing criminals, for instance. I'm surprised Dan doesn't do something about that."

Stephanie rolled her eyes, but kept on studying the poster in silence.

"As for rodeos," Roberta added, "I can't imagine why the town council thinks it's such a good idea. The Memorial Day festival has been around for years and managed perfectly well without adding something so utterly vulgar. Imagine all that dust and noise, not to mention the smell of those animals." She wrinkled her nose. "Disgusting. The fairgrounds will never be the same. Who wants to sit on grubby hard benches surrounded by screaming spectators watching a bunch of cowboys being flung to the ground? Bor-ing!" She stalked to the door, nose in the air. "You won't catch me anywhere near that place."

The door closed behind her, leaving only the heavy fragrance of Obsession hanging in the air.

Stephanie let out her breath on an exasperated sigh. "That . . . *woman.* I'd like to put her in an arena with a raging bull." She put down the poster and moved to the register, where she began entering Clara's purchase.

"She'd have the bull running back to the chutes with his tail between his legs." Clara dug in her purse for her credit card. "So what was the fight about earlier?"

Stephanie raised her eyebrows. "How'd you know about that?"

"I came in the door in the middle of it."

"I didn't see you."

"I know. I backed out when I saw you two facing off like a couple of territorial wolves."

"Coward."

"Yep, that's me." Clara swiped her card through the credit card machine. "So what was it about, anyway?"

Stephanie sighed. "Roberta had the brilliant idea for a joint promotion."

"A what?"

"Promotion. She wants to set up a tent on the sidewalk during the Memorial Day festival outside our two stores, with tables for our combined sale-priced merchandise."

Clara thought about it. "That might not be such a bad idea."

"The festival is this weekend. How are we supposed to put all that together in three days?"

"I guess it is a little short notice."

"She wanted to hire musicians, a juggler and a fortune-teller, among other just as stupid things."

Clara grinned. "A fortune-teller?"

Stephanie waved a hand at the model. "Like that. Crystal ball and everything. She said it would advertise all the weird stuff we sell."

"And what did you say to that?"

"I told her that there was no way I was going to participate in such outlandish commercialism. That our customers come to our store to quietly browse the shelves, enjoy a peaceful cup of coffee and a pastry in the Reading Nook and take all the time they want to make up their minds about what they'd like to buy."

Clara nodded. "But we did have a tarot card reader here last Christmas."

"She was tucked away in a corner, where people could consult her in private. She wasn't sitting in the middle of a bunch of musicians and a *juggler*."

Stephanie almost gagged on the last word, and Clara patted her shoulder. "Calm down. I'm sure you got your point across."

"You wouldn't believe the price she wanted us to pay for all that nonsense."

"Hmm. I can see why that made the idea even less appetizing."

"We couldn't afford it, for one thing. Even if I'd wanted to do it, which I don't." Stephanie shuddered. "Can you imagine—all that mess and noise blocking the sidewalk? I doubt if Dan would allow it, anyway."

"Did you tell Roberta that?"

"No. I told her I wasn't going to bulldoze our customers into buying our books."

"Ah. I guess she didn't much care for that."

"She went ballistic." Stephanie shook her head. "I think she was just mad that I wouldn't go along with her expensive, harebrained scheme. I don't get her. She'd use those kinds of tactics to get people into her store, yet she puts down the rodeo as vulgar and disgusting."

"In a way I have to agree with her. Rodeos are definitely not my thing."

"Then why are you so anxious to put up the poster?"

"I'm not anxious." Clara picked up the poster again. "I'm just doing a favor for Rick. One of the calf ropers is an old buddy of his." She stared at the garish photo of the rodeo clown that took up most of the page.

He wore black and white striped pants, a black and white checkered coat and a black vest with a splash of red beneath it. His face was white except for a bright red nose and large red circles around his eyes. Black lines spread out like spiderwebs across the circles and at the corners of his mouth, which had been painted with huge yellow lips.

A shiver slid down Clara's back. There was something about clowns that rattled her chains. She was about to put the poster down when suddenly the walls of the bookstore melted away. Recognizing the onslaught of a vision, she braced herself.

She was in the dark. Stars blinked at her from a black

sky, and only a sliver of a new moon looked down on her. The sound of a car engine split the silence with a dull roar, and she realized she was in a parking lot—one she didn't recognize. The smells of hamburgers and barbecue sauce wafted from a well-lit building on the far side.

The roar grew louder, then a figure appeared before her, running. As he turned his face in her direction she saw two red circles around his eyes and thick yellow lips, glowing in the faint light from the far-off streetlamp.

The next instant a truck caught up with him, plowed into him and threw him into the air. She heard his scream and shut her eyes, unwilling to watch him smash into the ground.

"Clara! Speak to me!"

Stephanie's urgent voice jerked her eyes open. She was back in the bookstore, the poster still trembling in her hands.

Her cousin's eyes gleamed with excitement. "It happened, didn't it? You had a vision. What was it?"

"Shhh!" Clara looked around in alarm, afraid someone would overhear. She had spent most of her life trying to hide the fact that she had inherited the family curse, as she called it. Many members of her family had some version of the Quinn Sense—a sixth sense that allowed them to interpret dreams, tell when someone was lying and occasionally see the future.

Clara's version was unpredictable, and was rarely there

when she needed it. The worst part of it were the visions, which popped up at the most awkward times, plunging her mind into the past or the future while her body remained, helpless, in the present.

Fortunately the episodes were usually brief, and she was able to attribute her odd behavior to a bout of indigestion. Her biggest fear was that someday she'd be "out" for so long her weird legacy would be revealed and people would consider her a freak. She couldn't bear the thought of having to explain it all to Rick.

Stephanie was the only one who knew Clara had the Quinn Sense, and she had been sworn to secrecy. Since neither of them had siblings, they had turned to each other for company, and had grown up practically joined at the hip. They had shared everything, from toys and clothes to their deepest secrets.

Stephanie had waited in vain to develop the Sense, and bitterly resented the fact that Clara had inherited it while she hadn't. Clara, on the other hand, would gladly give the wretched so-called gift to her cousin and be rid of it once and for all.

She met Stephanie's gaze and sighed. "Yes, I had a vision, but I don't know what it means."

"So what did you see?"

"It was this clown. It looked like he was being run down by a truck." She looked back at the poster and shuddered at the memory of the clown flying through the air.

"I just hope it's not an omen of something bad happening at the rodeo."

Stephanie pulled a face. "Doesn't something bad happen at every rodeo? I've never been to one, but I've seen bits of them on TV. There's an awful lot of men being tossed off horses and bulls and narrowly escaping being trampled to death."

Clara grinned. "Guess we're just not big fans of rodeo around here."

"I didn't say that." Stephanie picked up a handful of gift cards and began stacking them in a holder. "I think it would be fun—all those cowboy hunks showing off their muscles. I could go for that."

Clara pretended to be shocked. "That's no way for a married woman and mother of three to talk."

Stephanie leered at her. "A woman can dream, can't she?"

The doorbell jingled just then and Clara turned to see Rick in the doorway.

He looked relieved when he saw her. "Oh, great. You're still here. You took off so fast I didn't have time to ask you."

Anticipation made her tingle. They hadn't been dating long, and time spent with Rick was still new enough to be exciting. "Ask me what?"

He held up two tickets. "Come to the rodeo with me? Wes gave me free tickets and a promise of a tour if we got there early enough."

Clara could feel Stephanie's gaze on her. Having just declared her dislike of rodeos, she'd look like a hypocrite if she accepted Rick's offer. Then again, her cousin would totally understand why she couldn't turn down a date with him. "I'd love to go. When? What time?"

Before Rick could answer, the doorbell rang again, and Roberta sailed in. She was breathing a little hard, suggesting she'd made a mad dash to get into the bookstore before Rick left.

Gliding over to his side, she took the tickets from his fingers. "Oh, my," she purred. "Tickets for the rodeo! I just *adore* the rodeo. Are these for sale?"

Clara gritted her teeth.

To her relief, Rick plucked the tickets back. "Sorry, but these were a gift from a buddy, and I'm taking Clara."

Roberta raised her delicate eyebrows. "Really?" Her tone implied that Rick was making a grave mistake. "Too bad. I would have loved to see it. I don't suppose your friend has any more tickets floating around?"

"I'll ask him when I see him," Rick said, then turned his back on the woman. "These are for opening night. That's tomorrow. I'll pick you up from here. Can you get away early?"

Clara looked at Stephanie, who was frowning at Roberta as if she were putting a curse on her. "Okay with you, Steffie?"

Her cousin waved a careless hand at her. "Of course. I'll ask Molly to cover for you. She could use the overtime. She has her eye on a new car."

"Then I guess we're all set."

"Great!" He looked at Clara. "Five thirty work for you?"

She nodded, trying to ignore the dark looks Roberta sent her way. "I'll be ready."

Rick was halfway out the door when Roberta called out, "Oh, Ricky! I need to talk to you." She ran after him, slamming the door behind her.

Stephanie shook her head. "Does that woman ever give up?"

Clara laughed. "I doubt it. She's wasting her time. Rick's made it very plain he's not interested."

"Well, I shouldn't think so. You two obviously have a good thing going." She cupped a hand behind her ear. "Do I hear wedding bells sometime soon?"

"No, you don't. We barely know each other, and it's much too soon to even think about the future." Deciding it was time to talk about something else, Clara held up the poster. "Where shall we put this?"

Stephanie nodded at the window. "If you think you can crawl past all that stuff, it can go in there."

"I'll see what I can do."

It took her several minutes to weave her way through strands of beads, crystals swinging on silver strings and the stuffed raven perched on a large portrait of Edgar Allan Poe. Across the street she saw Roberta standing in front of Rick's store, barring him from entering. She was gesturing with her hand, gazing up at him while a torrent of words flowed through her lips.

Whatever she was saying apparently had no effect, since Rick placed his hands on her shoulders, gently moved her to one side and disappeared into the store.

Roberta paused for a moment, staring after him, then, with a toss of her head, marched back across the street to the stationer's.

Smiling, Clara unrolled the poster, trying not to look at the clown as she taped it to the window. A couple of passersby paused to watch, and she gave them a wave before scrambling back into the store.

"So," Stephanie said, as Clara joined her behind the counter, "you're going to sit on grubby hard benches surrounded by screaming spectators watching a bunch of cowboys being flung to the ground."

Clara punched her lightly on the arm. "Shut up. I'm going on a date with Rick. That's all that matters." And for the rest of the day, that's all she could think about.

She spent the afternoon running errands then took an enthusiastic Tatters for a walk on the beach. The big dog strained at his leash the moment they hit the sand, dragging Clara along behind him.

"Stop that!" She dug in her heels and hauled on the leash. "You know very well you can't run without a leash until after eight o'clock. It's the law."

Tatters turned his head to look back at her. *Poop on the law.*

Clara tightened her grip. She'd offered to take care of Tatters when Rick's ex-wife had dumped the dog on him.

As unnerving as it had been to discover she was able to read people's minds, nothing had prepared her for the shock of finding out she could read Tatters' thoughts. Or that he could understand every word spoken to him.

She had to restrain herself from answering him, knowing how ridiculous she looked holding a one-sided conversation with a dog. Instead she gave the leash a sharp, warning tug and prayed he'd behave.

To her relief he trotted along at her side, though every now and then he'd give a puff of frustration, his gaze on the seagulls circling overhead. Tatters loved nothing more than to charge down the beach, leaping and barking at the screeching gulls. Since that could only happen during the summer when the evening sky was lighter for longer, he made the most of it when given the opportunity.

Clara often wondered if he and the birds were actually having a verbal battle, flinging insults back and forth. If so, the seagulls were fighting a losing war.

By the time she arrived back home, her mother had started dinner.

When Clara had first left New York to return home, she'd moved in with her mother on a temporary basis, just until she found an apartment. The search had been more difficult than she'd anticipated. At first she'd resented her mother's constant probing into her private life, both past and present, but gradually she'd come to realize that Jessie was simply being a little overprotective, and genuinely cared about her daughter.

They'd managed to compromise. Clara was making an effort to be less secretive, and Jessie was striving to be less intrusive. There were still times when one or the other stepped over the mark, but things in the Quinn household were a lot less tense than they had been—to the point where Clara no longer scanned the *TO RENT* columns in the *Harbor Chronicle* or combed through the ads on craigslist.

The moment she opened the front door, her mother yelled from the kitchen, "Wipe that dog's feet before he comes in here!"

Tatters uttered a low, threatening growl, and Clara quickly laid a hand on his neck. "Down, boy. Give me your paw."

Tatters lifted a front leg and Clara checked it out. The walk back had dislodged most of the sand, and she brushed off what was left. After a few grunts from the dog, and a soft warning from her, his paws were clean enough to satisfy Jessie.

Clara walked into the kitchen with Tatters at her heels. Her mother stood at the stove with a stir-fry sizzling in front of her. The smell of ginger and peppers reminded Clara she was hungry. "Need any help?"

Jessie glanced over her shoulder. "You can set the table for me, if you like."

"Sure." Clara walked over to the counter and opened a cabinet door. "Before I forget, I won't be here for dinner tomorrow night."

"Going out with Rick?"

"Uh-huh. He's taking me to the rodeo."

"Oh, I heard about it on the news. They had to renovate the fairgrounds for it. I hope they get their money back." Jessie turned, a spatula gripped in her hand. "I didn't know you liked the rodeo."

"I don't." Clara took down a couple of dinner plates. "At least, I've never been to one. I know they have them occasionally in Maine, but I always thought it was more a Western thing. I like horses, though, so it should be okay."

"And Rick will be there," Jessie said slyly.

Clara was about to answer when a flash of light almost blinded her. Blinking, she found herself sitting on a hard bench, the sun full in her eyes. *Not again*, she thought, as she lifted a hand to shade her face from the glare. Two visions in one day was a little much.

In front of her she saw a huge arena, covered in sawdust. The seats were empty, the stands quiet. She was completely alone.

No, not quite. A movement to her right, high up in the stands, caught her eye. It was a figure in a black striped jacket and black and white checkered pants. He turned to look at her. Huge red circles surrounded his eyes, and a big red nose gleamed in the sunlight. He lifted a hand to wave at her, then, to her dismay, he slowly toppled forward and started bouncing headfirst down the stands.

An almighty crash made her jump. Her mother's voice,

high-pitched with alarm, demanded, "Clara? What the devil is the matter with you?"

Clara blinked again as the sunlight faded. She was back in the kitchen, pieces of a broken dinner plate lying at her feet and her mother's horrified gaze on her face.

2

Although Jessie had learned about the Quinn Sense from Clara's father, so far her daughter had managed to hide from her mother the fact that she had inherited the gift. Jessie was the last person in the world Clara wanted to know her secret. Her mother was a born gossip, and Clara was certain the news would be passed along to all Jessie's cronies. It would only be a matter of time before Rick heard about it.

She had come close to being discovered more than once, but never this close. Staring down at the broken plate, she muttered, "I'm so sorry. It just slipped from my hands."

Jessie frowned. "You're not usually this clumsy. Are you feeling all right? For a moment there you looked as if you were in some kind of trance."

"Heartburn, that's all. I need to eat." She dropped to her knees and began picking up the pieces.

"Wait! You'll cut yourself." Jessie reached under the counter for a dustpan and brush. "Here. Use this."

Clara took it from her, trying to curb her resentment. She wished, fervently, that she could be rid of the Sense once and for all. It was ruining her life. Bending her knees, she began swiping the broken pieces into the dustpan.

Tatters got up from his mat, strolled over to her and pushed his nose into her arm.

Looking into his eyes, Clara murmured, "Thanks, Tats. I'm okay."

"Tats?" Jessie sounded shocked. "Do you young people have to abbreviate every name you hear? You wouldn't believe how many people call me Jess. It makes me sound like a board game."

Clara straightened. "Actually, it's a sign they like you. Like a show of affection."

Jessie sniffed. "I can think of better ways to show affection."

Clara had to smile at that. Tipping the broken pieces into the trash can, she said, "I'll buy you a new plate tomorrow."

"Don't bother." Jessie reached up for another plate. "I never liked this set, anyway. I'll get out the best dishes. It's time we used them instead of keeping them hidden away."

Clara took the plate from her mother. "But they were a wedding present from Grandma. You only use those on special occasions."

Jessie smiled. "Every time I have dinner with you, it's a special occasion. You were gone for ten years in New York and I hardly saw you at all. Someday soon you'll be announcing you're getting married, and you'll be gone again. So I might as well make the most of the time I have with you now."

Clara could feel her cheeks growing warm. "What makes you think I'm getting married?"

"Your face when you come home from a date with Rick." Jessie turned back to her stir-fry. "I've never seen you look like that before."

Deciding there was no answer for her mother's observation, Clara set the plates down on the kitchen table. "If we start using the best china we should eat in the dining room. We haven't done that since Dad died."

"We haven't had dinner guests since your father died." Jessie glanced over her shoulder at Clara. "How about inviting Rick here for dinner some night?"

It wasn't the first time Jessie had suggested she invite Rick for dinner. So far Clara had managed to avoid the issue. She knew it was only a matter of time before she would have to either give in or deal with a barrage of questions from her mother.

In spite of Jessie's good intentions, she would no doubt

want to know every intimate detail about Rick's life, both past and present. She'd be interrogating him all through the evening, and Clara wasn't ready to face that embarrassment.

"We'll see," she said, and rummaged noisily in the cutlery drawer, hoping to distract her mother.

Jessie must have taken the hint, as she said no more, and Clara was able to enjoy a fairly peaceful meal. She offered to do the dishes while her mother settled in front of the TV to watch the news.

When Clara walked out of the kitchen, Jessie waved a hand at her. "Look at this. They're talking about the rodeo."

Clara gave the TV a wary glance. So far, whenever she'd seen a picture of the rodeo or it had been mentioned in detail, her mind had been whisked away somewhere. She was very much afraid that the clown in the poster was in danger, and she felt obligated to warn him. She just couldn't figure out how to do that. Even if she could explain how she knew he was in harm's way, it was totally unlikely he would believe her.

It was a problem she'd faced more than once in the past, and no matter what she did, the outcome had usually been awkward at best and downright unnerving at times.

Rick had told her that Wes had offered them a tour before the show. Perhaps, if she met the clown, she could say something that would put him on his guard. Considering how she felt about clowns, she was looking forward to that possibility with a certain amount of dread.

———

"Clara's going to the rodeo tomorrow," Stephanie said, nodding at the TV. The video of a cowboy thrashing around on the back of a bull was accompanied by roars of approval from the spectators in the stands, while blaring country music tried to drown them out.

Her husband sat on the couch next to her, apparently oblivious to the noise. His focus was on the phone in his hand, which emitted burps and bleeps with annoying regularity. So intense was his concentration, he failed to acknowledge his wife's comment.

Stephanie leaned over and punched him in the arm.

The phone squawked, and George looked up. "You killed my avatar."

Stephanie compressed her lips for a moment. "I didn't kill anything, but if you keep ignoring me for that silly phone that might change."

George sighed and leaned back. "Sorry. I was trying to relax my brain. It's been a tough day."

"How about relaxing it with some intelligent conversation?"

George looked around the room. "Your father is here?"

She punched him on the arm again. "Enough of the smart mouth. I want to talk about the rodeo."

"What rodeo?"

Stephanie looked at the TV, only to see a news story about a protest at the town hall. "It was on the news just now. Clara's going."

"Good for her."

"I'd like to go."

"Why?"

"Because I think it would be fun."

"For whom?"

She sighed. "You don't like rodeos?"

"I don't dislike them. I just think that if we're going to fork out money for babysitters, there are better places I'd rather take you." He stretched his arms over his head and yawned. "Like a fancy romantic restaurant and a movie?"

She thought about it. "We could take the kids."

"Seriously? You want to sit in the stands at the fairgrounds for two and a half hours watching the kids fight over seats, beg for ice cream, throw popcorn at one another and—"

"Okay, okay," Stephanie broke in. "It was just an idea."

"A bad one."

"So we're not going to the rodeo?"

"Why don't you go with Clara?"

"She's going with Rick."

"Ah." George nodded as if he'd just realized something important. "Those two getting serious?"

Stephanie shrugged. "I have no idea. Clara doesn't talk about it much."

George gave her a sympathetic look. "What you mean is she won't answer your probing questions."

"Something like that."

George reached out and pulled her close. "How about you and I plan a date night out? Somewhere quiet and romantic? Anywhere you want to go."

Stephanie smiled. "Now I know why I married you." She snuggled closer to her husband. Who needed a rodeo when she had all she really needed right there next to her? She pictured Clara sitting in the stands with Rick. That was what she wanted for her cousin—the kind of happiness she had with George.

Clara had some issues, though, that could ruin everything. What happened to her in New York had changed her. She had trouble trusting people. Then there was the Quinn Sense, making her feel like a freak. Yep, Clara had some work to do before she could be really happy.

"Is that a sigh of happiness, I hope?" George asked, breaking into her thoughts.

"Of course." She grinned up at him. "Now, where shall we go for our date night?"

The following afternoon Clara had trouble concentrating on anything. Molly had happily agreed to stay and close up the bookstore. Almost ten years younger than Clara, the energetic redhead was into new clothes, makeup and a vast collection of CDs, all of which took money, so she usually jumped at the chance to make a little extra pay.

"I have tickets for the rodeo, too," she said, when she learned why Clara needed the time off. "I'm going with Brad. You remember him—he worked up on the construction site."

"Of course I remember." Clara smiled. Molly had talked about little else for weeks. "What's he doing now that the new resort hotel is open?"

"He was working at the fairgrounds, handling the stuff they needed done for the rodeo." Molly's pretty face clouded over. "Now that's finished, Brad will have to find work on another construction site, and it's not likely to be in Finn's Harbor."

"Well, I'm sure he'll look for something close by."

Molly stared gloomily at the pile of cookbooks displayed on a table near the door. "He might look, but that doesn't mean he'll find something."

A customer passed by them, heading for the counter with three books under her arm. Saved from answering Molly, Clara hurried over to the cash register. She felt sorry for her friend. Construction jobs were hard to find in the coastal areas of Maine.

After chatting a few moments with her customer, Clara scanned the books and bagged them. Handing them over, she glanced at the clock. Another five hours to go before her date. It was going to be a long afternoon.

Time dragged as she restocked shelves, talked to a

sales rep and tidied up displays. A few tourists strolled in, but they were mostly lookers. Most of their regular customers visited the bookstore in the mornings, when the coffee was brewing and a plate of donuts and pastries awaited them in the Reading Nook. The afternoons were generally quiet. In the winter months hardly anyone shopped on Main Street after dark, but now that the tourist season had begun, more visitors wandered in during the evening hours.

Clara had just finished serving a customer when Rick walked through the door. Surprised that the last hour had snuck up on her, she greeted him with a hasty wave of her hand. "Be right with you!"

He nodded in answer and strolled over to the cookbook table. Watching him out of the corner of her eye, Clara had to smile. Rick loved to cook, and had served up a couple of great meals for her. He was always on the look-out for new recipes and different ideas for dinners.

She grabbed her purse and went looking for Molly, who was down one of the aisles helping a customer find the newest book in the Hunger Games series. After telling her she was leaving, Clara joined Rick at the front of the store.

"Ready to go watch some bucking broncos?" he asked, opening the door with a grin.

She wasn't, but she nodded anyway. "Lead on, Macduff."

"Ah, Shakespeare, I believe."

"Not exactly." She stepped out into the street, and waited for him to join her. "Actually, the correct quote is 'Lay on, Macduff.' It was spoken by Macbeth, when he refused to quit fighting and challenged Macduff to fight to the death. So originally the phrase meant to go to battle. Someone changed it along the way and now it means lead and I will follow."

Rick raised his eyebrows as they started down the hill. "Wow, I'm impressed."

"Don't be. It's one of the few bits of literary knowledge I own. Stephanie is the whiz kid of books. She practically grew up with her head in one."

Rick laughed. "But you work in the bookstore. You must know something about the books."

"Not as much as I should, I guess. I'm not a huge fan of the paranormal stuff. I do like to read, but my taste runs more into a good thriller, or maybe a hard-boiled mystery. Especially the classics."

"A Dashiell Hammett fan?"

"Absolutely."

"Ah, so that's why you like playing detective."

"I don't get involved intentionally. Somehow these things just happen."

"Well, whatever the reason, you saved my neck once and I'll always be in your debt for that."

She smiled, remembering the time Rick had been accused of murder. In order to help clear his name, she and Stephanie had launched a full-blown investigation, much to the disgust and irritation of Dan Petersen, Finn's Harbor's stalwart police chief. He'd been only slightly appeased when the cousins had helped solve the crime, since it wasn't the first time they had "interfered in police business," as he put it.

Exchanging a warm glance with Rick, she said lightly, "You've done some rescuing of your own in the past. In fact, you always seem to turn up at the right moment whenever I'm in danger."

"Then let's call it even."

"Done." She turned her face to the sun. Most of the tourists had disappeared, no doubt enjoying dinner somewhere. The light breeze from the sea below drifted up to cool her skin. This was the time of year she loved best—before the sultry heat of summer made walking a misery of sweat and fatigue.

They reached the parking lot where Rick's truck was parked. He'd cracked the windows, but the sun had heated the cab, and Clara inched onto the leather seat, conscious of the warmth through her light cotton capris.

Once they were on the coast road the air conditioner kicked in, and by the time they reached the turn heading inland, she felt comfortably cool.

During the ten minutes it took to get to the fairgrounds, they had a lively discussion on the differences between the early hard-boiled mysteries and the contemporary ones. They both finally agreed that it was all a matter of taste, and had switched to talking about the new Hill Top

Resort by the time they arrived at the fairgrounds where the rodeo was being held.

Rick parked the truck and opened the door for her to climb out. "Wes told me to ask for him at the box office. It's over there." He nudged his head at a booth that stood near the entrance.

Clara followed him, taking in her surroundings. She had been to the fairgrounds many times. The Memorial Day weekend festival had been held each year since long before she was born. She and Stephanie had looked forward to it every spring, originally with their parents, then later by themselves—until Clara had left to attend college in New York in a vain attempt to escape the infamous Quinn curse, as she called it.

She was teaching students with the intention of becoming a professor when she met Matt. She fell hard, and when he proposed, she was quick to accept. On the evening of her wedding she was devastated to learn he'd left town with his young assistant. She'd returned to Finn's Harbor, and it had taken her over a year to come to terms with her mistake.

Even now, she felt an ache when an unbidden memory surfaced, which prodded her to take things slowly with Rick. She had been so sure of Matt, and even the Quinn Sense hadn't warned her of his betrayal. Or maybe it had and she just hadn't listened, which would account for the fact that she had told no one, not even her mother, that she'd planned to get married.

Glancing at Rick's sturdy shoulders, she felt warmth erasing the memories. Rick was a far cry from the man who had treated her so badly. She was happy to be with him, and happy to be sharing this first performance of what would probably be an annual event at the Memorial Day festival.

Prepared to see big changes to the fairgrounds, at first all she could see was the familiar large building that housed the merchandise vendors. As usual, a scattering of booths alongside offered cotton candy, ice cream and soft pretzels, among other tasty snacks.

As they rounded the corner of the building, she could see the arena and the stands. The sight reminded her of her vision, and she suppressed her shiver of apprehension. The original stadium, often used for sporting events, had been widened, and she could see where a row of chutes had been added in front of the entrance.

Clara's pulse quickened. She wasn't sure how she felt about the evening's entertainment. Watching men risk their necks on the backs of angry bulls wasn't exactly her idea of a good time. Yet she couldn't ignore the tingle of anticipation at the thought. It would be interesting, to say the least.

Apparently Rick had been given some directions by his friend, as he beckoned to her and started walking toward the chutes. She followed, trying not to think about a chubby clown tumbling headfirst down the steps.

On the other side of the arena stood a large stage where

concerts were held. Clara smiled, thinking of the warm nights she and her cousin had sat listening to the music of local bands hoping to make it big.

The aroma of smoked meats and barbecue sauce wafting from the food tent made her feel hungry. She dodged between spectators, some of whom munched on corn dogs and pretzels, while others carried tubs of popcorn and cups of beer.

As she approached the back of the chutes, the stink of sawdust and manure made her forget about food. Reaching a large fenced area, she paused next to Rick and gazed at the men in jeans, checkered shirts and cowboy hats trotting around on horseback.

"Welcome to the warm-up corral," a voice said behind them.

Clara spun around.

The man facing them wore a wide-brimmed hat pulled down over his forehead. Blue eyes in a darkly tanned face smiled at her. "You must be Clara. I've heard a lot about you."

Clara smiled back. "I hope it was complimentary."

"Yes, ma'am. You'd be flattered, I promise."

"This is Wes," Rick said hurriedly, sounding a bit rattled. "He's going to show us around. Right?"

This last was directed at the cowboy, with a warning scowl.

Wes's grin widened. "Sure. Follow me." He fell into step beside Clara as they walked toward the holding pens. "So how long have you been dating Crafty?"

Clara glanced at him. "Who?"

On the other side of her, Rick grunted. "It was my nickname in high school."

"Oh! Is that where you guys met?"

"Yeah." He exchanged glances with Wes. "We met our freshman year and graduated together."

"Crafty?" Clara raised her eyebrows at Rick. "Was that a compliment, or were you devious when you were young?"

"It's not what you think."

Wes laughed. "We called him that because he was the best craftsman in the class. When the rest of us were goofing off our senior year, he spent most of his time in woodshop."

Intrigued, she wanted to ask them more about their high school days, but decided this probably wasn't a good time. They'd reached an area fenced off into several squares, with large gates at one end.

"This is the rough stock area," Wes said, waving at the empty stalls. "This is where the broncs and bulls wait to go into the arena. They'll be out here soon." He pointed at the gates. "See how sturdy they are? When those are opened, they form a safe passageway for the stock to pass through to the chutes." He looked at Rick. "You've heard of the world's most dangerous bull?"

Rick nodded. "Bodacious. He was around in the nineties, right?"

"Right. That bull could leap six feet in the air with all

four feet off the ground. He was wily as a fox—used to buck his riders forward, then bring his head up to smash into their faces. More than one rider ended up with a broken nose. That bull was one mean dude."

"No kidding."

"Yeah, well, we've got one of his offspring. Ferocious. Just as mean. Make sure you keep out of his way."

Clara shivered. It was unlike anything she'd experienced before. She could imagine the bull, snorting and stamping impatiently while he waited for his turn. Looking at the gates, she hoped Wes was right and they were strong enough to hold a raging bull if things got out of hand.

Wes was talking about the bronc riders, and how some used saddles and some rode bareback. He paused to wave at a couple of women strolling by, explaining that they were barrel racers. "You gotta know how to really handle a horse in that event," he said, watching the two women depart. "It's fast-paced, and a lot depends on the horse's strength and ability. Those gals gotta know how to follow the pattern and hug that barrel as they go around it."

Clara concentrated on what he was saying, beginning to feel a tingle of excitement at the prospect of watching the competition. "It sounds dangerous."

Wes grinned. "That's what puts the thrill in it. It's a spectator sport, and you gotta give the public something for their money. Trust me, those racers are a lot tougher than they look. They're good at what they do."

Clara was about to answer him when another voice spoke from behind her. "Don't listen to him, hon. He's full of BS."

Clara turned, and felt a chill chase all the way down her back. She was looking into the painted face of the clown in the poster. Seen in real life, he looked even more formidable. Dark eyes stared out at her from the red circles and the web of lines drawn inside them. His yellow lips looked huge and deformed, and his red nose gleamed against the mask of white paint that covered the rest of his face. He wore the same outfit he wore in the poster, with his black cowboy hat pushed to the back of his head. "Didn't mean to give you a start, little lady."

Realizing that she was staring at him with something like horror on her face, Clara quickly transformed her expression. "I didn't see you there."

"Meet Marty Pearce," Wes said. "Also known as Sparky the clown. He entertains the crowd while they wait for the next event." He looked at the clown. "This is Clara and Rick. They're good friends of mine, so be nice."

"I'm always nice." Marty held out a white-gloved hand to Clara and bowed. "I'm privileged to make your acquaintance, ma'am."

Clara tried not to shiver as she hastily shook the hand and let it go.

Wes rolled his eyes. "He never does anything half-assed."

"I'll take that as a compliment." The dark eyes seemed

to penetrate right through Clara's skull. "I hope you're staying for the performance?"

"Yes, I'm looking forward to it." Clara gulped. A vision of the clown's body flying through the air had flashed through her mind. Was she about to watch Sparky the clown being gored by a bull? Desperately she sought for words to warn him, yet could think of nothing to say that wouldn't make her sound like a raving lunatic.

As if reading her mind, Wes said, "Don't expect him to chase after a bull. He gave that up a while ago. He just keeps the kids entertained now."

Clara thought she saw a spark of resentment in the dark eyes, but it was gone so fast she figured she'd imagined it. Still, she felt obliged to say something nice. "Well, I'll enjoy being entertained."

Marty's whole face broke into a grin. "Thank you, kind lady. I'll be sure and wave to you when I'm out there entertaining the crowd." He nodded at Rick. "Nice to have met you, sir. I hope you enjoy the show."

"I'm sure we will." Rick looked amused as Marty wandered off. "He seems like a nice guy."

"Yeah." Wes tipped the brim of his hat back with his thumb. "He used to be a bullfighter—it's what we call the clowns who distract the bulls when the riders come off them. But Marty got in the way of a bull's horns once too often. He was in a hospital for weeks. Now he just fills in the gaps in between events. The crowds love him. He's a great entertainer."

"He misses performing with the bulls," Clara said.

Wes looked surprised. "Yeah, I guess he does."

Rick gave her an odd look, but said nothing as Wes added, "I gotta go and get stuff ready for the show. See you later?"

"Sure." Rick clapped a hand on the cowboy's shoulder. "Good to see you, buddy. Thanks for the tour."

"Yes, thanks," Clara added hastily. "I really enjoyed it."

Wes grinned. "A pleasure, ma'am." With a wave at them both, he hurried off, leaving them to find their way back to the arena.

Rick took Clara's hand and tucked it under his arm. "How do you do that?"

She looked at him, immediately on guard. "Do what?"

"Know what people are feeling or thinking."

She managed a fairly convincing laugh. "I don't. It's just guesswork."

"Pretty good guesswork if you ask me. No wonder you're so good at detecting."

They were on dangerous ground, and she quickly changed the subject. "I'm starving. Can we eat?"

Rick grinned. "There you go again, reading my mind."

Fortunately they'd reached the entrance to the tent, and she was saved from answering.

The smell of hot dogs and hamburgers filled the warm, sticky air inside. Rick headed for a stand near the back of the tent, where a couple of young women were serving chicken wraps.

"Look good to you?" he asked, and she nodded. Right then she would have eaten anything he put in her hand.

They found a vacant table and Clara sat down with the wraps while Rick wandered off in search of the beer booth. He came back moments later with two cups brimming with ice-cold beer. "Now this," he said, as he sat down opposite her, "is what I call dining in style."

She gave him a lopsided smile. "Obviously, you don't get out much."

"I have my moments." He reached across the table to squeeze her hand. "And this is one of them."

She squeezed back, feeling a rush of pleasure at the warmth in his eyes. "I'm glad you're having a good time."

"Aren't you?"

"Of course!" She wished she could be more enthusiastic, but the dread lurking in the back of her mind dampened her spirits. She couldn't shake the feeling that she was going to witness something bad happening to Sparky the clown.

The feeling stayed with her throughout the performance. The pageantry of the opening parade impressed her. Women in glittering vests and chaps cantered into the arena bearing flags and were followed by cowboys on horseback twirling lassos. She couldn't contain a shiver, however, at the sight of the clowns tumbling alongside.

Sparky brought up the rear of the parade, juggling bright yellow and red clubs that he constantly dropped, sometimes on his head, which brought shouts of laughter from the younger members of the audience.

As time went by, Clara sat on the edge of her seat as one competitor after another hit the sawdust hard. It amazed her that they all scrambled to their feet, apparently unhurt by the violent contact with the ground. She enjoyed the barrel racing, but watching the clowns being chased by the hefty bulls made her mouth go dry. Between each event Sparky appeared in the arena, telling jokes or turning clumsy cartwheels, bursting balloons and making the audience giggle.

During the intermission, he performed a lengthy routine, which involved pretending to be chased by someone dressed up as a two-legged bull. Sparky ended up in the stands, hiding behind various children, amid shrieks and screams of laughter.

Apparently the clown's antics didn't impress Rick, as he took off to get more drinks, leaving Clara alone to watch the show. She was surprised when she saw Wes loping up the steps toward her, his bright red shirt a splash of color among the crowd. "Rick's gone to get a beer," she explained as Wes took the empty seat next to her. She checked her watch. "He should be back any minute."

Wes nodded. "I just came up to see how you're both enjoying the show."

"It's great!" Clara tried to sound genuinely excited rather than nervous and preoccupied. "I loved the barrel racing. Those women really know how to ride."

"They sure do." Wes stretched his long legs out in front of him. "I don't know what's wrong with Marty tonight, though. He seems off his game."

Clara stared at him. "He is? But the audience seems to love him."

"Yeah, but he's not putting a hundred percent into it like he usually does. I tried to talk to him earlier, but he took off before I could say anything. Guess he's feeling under the weather tonight. Happens to the best of us."

Uneasiness rippled through Clara's body. If Sparky was sick, maybe that's why she kept seeing him in trouble. "I'm sorry to hear that. It must be hard to act funny when you're not feeling good."

"Yeah." Wes rose to his feet as Rick appeared on the steps. "Well, enjoy the rest of the show."

"Thanks. I know we will." She watched him pause to speak to Rick, then he disappeared into the group of people below.

Rick handed her a cup of beer and sat down. "Wes is in the next-to-last event. Calf roping. You'll enjoy that."

Clara took a sip of the cold beer. "I'm looking forward to seeing your friend compete." She actually did enjoy it, once Rick assured her that the calves were not hurt. It was easy to pick out Wes in his red shirt, and she applauded with enthusiasm when he won the event.

When Marty's last turn in the arena ended without mishap she finally relaxed. Maybe her visions were simply about him not feeling well—like he was coming down with a cold or something. It didn't seem as if he was in actual danger, though she found it impossible to totally let go of her anxiety until the final parade wound its way around the ring amid tumultuous applause from the crowd.

"You can unclench your teeth now," Rick said, as they filed down the steps behind a group of chattering kids.

"Thanks." She gave him a rueful smile. "Was I that obvious?"

He grabbed her hand as they reached the walkway. "No, not really. I could tell you weren't exactly lapping it up, though."

"Sorry. I did enjoy parts of it, but I guess I was afraid someone would get hurt."

"Nothing wrong with having a soft heart. I like that."

She gave his fingers a grateful squeeze. They had reached the ground now. Their seats had been on the opposite side of the arena, near the concert stage. Clara gazed at it as they passed, remembering how it looked with a glowing backdrop and lights, lasers flashing and musicians writhing in front of the microphones.

Without warning her thoughts were shattered as a piercing scream rang out above the chatter of the crowd.

Rick halted, pulling her to a stop. "What the heck was that?"

More screams erupted, and now the people in front of them were turning toward the stage, muttering to one another.

Clara was closest to the corner of the stage. Staring into the darkness she saw a teenage couple rush out from behind the structure. The girl was crying, waving her arms, sobbing out words that Clara couldn't understand.

Her boyfriend shouted, "Somebody call 911! There's a dead body back there!"

Rick muttered something unintelligible, and Clara stood rooted to the spot, once more seeing the body of Sparky the clown tumbling headfirst down the steep rows of the stands. It was her fault. She should have warned him. Now Marty Pearce was dead and it was too late to save him.

3

Clara slept badly that night and woke up to find Tatters pawing her arm. "Sorry, boy," she muttered, as she clambered out of bed and reached for her robe. "I guess you need to go out."

Tatters grunted and trotted over to the door. Clara opened it for him and followed him down the hallway to the kitchen.

Seated at the table with a newspaper spread out in front of her, Jessie looked up. "Oh, there you are. I was just about to bring you a cup of coffee." She narrowed her eyes. "You look miserable. You must have had a bad night."

"I did." Clara opened the back door, and Tatters rushed outside. "Have you seen any news about the murder?"

"Murder?" Jessie picked up the newspaper. "What murder?"

"At the rodeo last night. I don't know too much about it, but from what we heard, someone found a dead body behind the concert stage."

"No kidding!" Jessie turned the pages. "Oh, here it is! I'm surprised it didn't make the front page." She began reading aloud. "The opening performance of Finn's Harbor's fledgling rodeo was marred by the discovery of a dead body. Lisa Warren, assistant to production manager Paul Eastcott, was found strangled to death. The police are investigating, and so far there are no suspects. This is the first time the Hometown Rodeo Company has visited Finn's Harbor, and Mr. Eastcott has expressed his deep regret to the patrons for the unfortunate beginning to the six-day event."

Clara walked over to the coffeepot and poured herself a cup. Before the security guards had ushered them out last night, she'd overheard rumors that the victim was a young woman. It had been a relief of sorts to know it wasn't Marty Pearce.

Carrying her coffee, Clara walked over to the table and sat down. The Sense had been trying to tell her something, however. Since Lisa Warren hadn't appeared in any of her visions, the young woman couldn't have been the one being warned. Clara had a bad feeling that Marty was still in danger. Maybe from the same person who had killed the production assistant. Somehow she had to find a way to warn him.

"So how was your date with Rick?" Jessie picked up the newspaper again and tried to look indifferent.

Clara wasn't fooled. Her mother avidly waited for details after every date. "It was great. I didn't think I would enjoy the rodeo, but it turned out to be a lot more fun than I'd expected. Though I have to admit, watching the clowns being chased by an angry bull was a little unsettling."

Jessie smiled. "You've always hated clowns. I remember one birthday party when your father insisted on hiring one. You and Stephanie hid in your bedroom closet and refused to come out until the clown left."

Clara shivered. "There was something weird about that clown."

"All clowns are weird, darling. That's part of their getup. Did Rick enjoy the show?"

"Yes, he did. I think rodeos are more a guy thing, anyway."

Jessie laughed. "You may be right." She glanced up at the cuckoo clock on the wall. The clock had belonged to Clara's great grandmother, and the cuckoo had been silenced with age, much to Clara's relief. "Oh, goodness. Is that the time?" Jessie folded the newspaper and stood. "I suppose you'll be working late, as usual?"

"I'll be home soon after eight."

"I'll make a salad." Jessie reached the door and looked

back at her. "Try not to worry about the murder, darling. Let the police handle it. I can't for the life of me imagine what you find so fascinating about solving murders, but you do tend to run into trouble when you get involved."

Clara nodded. If only it were that simple. She couldn't ignore her visions, especially if they could help find a killer. "Have a good day, Mom."

Jessie sighed. "You, too."

On her way to the Raven's Nest later, Clara tried to put the conversation out of her mind, but the memory of Sparky the clown tumbling through the air refused to go away. Stephanie pounced on her the moment she entered the bookstore, which didn't help matters.

"So what happened last night?" Stephanie demanded. "Did you hear about the murder? Did you see anything?"

Clara dumped her purse behind the counter and smiled at a customer waving at her from one of the aisles. "No, I didn't see anything. All I know is what's in the *Chronicle*."

Her cousin looked disappointed. "Oh, I thought you would have at least tried to get a peek at the body."

"Nope. The security guards were there in seconds. Besides, I've sworn off chasing after killers."

"Since when?"

"Since I nearly got killed by one."

Stephanie pulled a face. "I just thought you'd want to know what was going on."

"I'll watch the news."

Giving up, Stephanie switched subjects. "So what did you think of the rodeo? Did you get to meet the cowboys?"

"I met Wes, Rick's pal." Clara picked up an invoice and studied it. "And I met Sparky the clown."

Stephanie raised her eyebrows. "Really? The one on the poster?"

"Yep." Clara tried to ignore the little flutter of apprehension.

"You didn't run away from him?"

"No, I didn't. I've grown up since that birthday party."

"You still don't like clowns."

"Neither do you."

"So what's he like?"

"Nice. Harmless. Friendly." Clara waved the invoice at her. "So Jane Rancher's next fantasy book is in. We've got four customers waiting for that one."

"I know." Stephanie took the invoice from her. "I was going to pull the copies from one of the boxes but haven't had time. Can you take care of it?"

"Sure." Clara glanced at the clock. "Don't you have a dentist appointment?"

"Crap. I'm already late!" Stephanie rummaged under the counter for her purse. "Call me tonight?"

"Don't I always?"

Grinning, Stephanie rushed to the door and opened it. "You haven't said anything about your date with Rick."

Clara sighed. "I'll tell you everything tonight."

Apparently satisfied, Stephanie left.

Moments later, just as Clara was on her way to the stockroom, the door opened again and Rick walked in. His usual cheery grin was absent, and he greeted her with a heavy tone that boded trouble.

She walked over to him, glancing over her shoulder to make sure no one was nearby. "What's wrong?"

He moved closer to her, muttering in a low voice, "Wes has been taken in for questioning. They think he killed that woman last night."

Clara let out her breath in a rush of dismay. "Oh no. I'm sorry, Rick."

He shook his head. "He didn't do it. Wes is like a brother to me. I know him. He'd never hurt anyone intentionally, much less kill someone."

Clara struggled to find words to reassure him. "Well, if he's innocent, Dan will know it and let him go. He's a good police chief."

"I hope so. Even good cops make mistakes. I know that for a fact."

Seeing the pain in his eyes, she laid a hand on his arm. It wasn't that long ago that he'd been under suspicion of murder, and questioned by the police himself. He'd gone through untold misery until his name had been cleared.

"Try not to worry. I'm sure things will work out all right. How did you find out about Wes?"

Rick gave her fingers a grateful squeeze. "I ran into

Tim and asked him about the murder. He told me Wes was at the station being questioned."

"Why do they think Wes killed that woman?"

"They found Wes's pigging string wrapped around her neck."

"His *what* string?"

"Pigging string. It's what the calf ropers use to tie down a calf after they've wrestled it to the ground. Some of them are distinctive. Wes's was handmade—red, white and blue—the only one like it in the rodeo."

Clara shook her head. "Surely that can't be enough to arrest him? Anyone could have taken it and used it."

"That's what I told Tim, but he said that Wes couldn't account for half an hour of his time last night. What's more, a couple of the barrel racers said they heard him fighting with Lisa earlier that afternoon."

Anxious to take away his look of despair, Clara tried again. "Police need proof before they can bring charges. They'll test DNA and—"

"And Wes's DNA will be all over the pigging string."

"So will that of whoever killed her."

"Maybe." Rick looked unconvinced. "Anyway, I'd better get back to the store. Tyler's waiting to go on a break."

She watched him go, wishing she could have said something to take that look off his face. Walking back to the stockroom, she thought about the tour Wes had given them. She'd liked the charismatic cowboy, and it was hard to visualize him as a ruthless killer.

Still, she knew from past experience how dumb it was to judge a book by its cover. She'd been fooled before by a friendly face and a captivating manner. All she could hope was that Dan was wrong about Wes and the real killer would soon be caught.

She opened the door to the stockroom and switched on the light. There was a small window at the back of the room, but it never gave enough illumination to read the labels on the boxes. Stephanie had stacked the ones she wanted opened in the middle of the room, and Clara walked over to the pile, curious to see the new books that had arrived that morning.

Just as she reached for the first one, a soft sound made her pause. She lifted her head, listening intently. It wasn't the first time she'd heard an odd sound in the stockroom, but she'd never been able to figure out where it was coming from.

As always, the sound wasn't repeated, and, shaking her head, she took her box cutter out of her pocket.

The next instant she was out in the evening sun. Dusk was settling all around her, and a familiar smell hung in the air. Horses. She was at the rodeo, standing behind some kind of structure—the concert stage.

Her nerves jumped as she saw a figure lying on the ground. The woman's long, dark hair dragged in the dust, and someone in a red shirt and jeans stood over her, holding a thin, brightly colored rope.

Clara blinked, trying to recognize the lean cowboy. He had his back to her, and his cowboy hat hid his head. One thing she did know. As far as she could remember, Wes was the only contestant wearing a red shirt that night. Things were not looking good for Rick's high school buddy.

Later that afternoon, Tim Rossi wandered into the store and waved at Clara as he headed for the aisles. Tim rarely bought anything. He was more interested in whatever snacks were left over in the Reading Nook.

This time, however, he returned to the counter carrying a book. "I never thought my mother would be interested in fantasy," he said, as he handed Clara the book. "She's really happy you recommended this series."

Clara smiled. "I'm glad she's enjoying it. There's a couple more on the shelves when she's finished this one."

Tim swiped his credit card and put it back in his wallet. "Rick said you were at the rodeo last night. What did you think of it?"

"I enjoyed it more than I thought I would." She hesitated, wondering if she should bring up the subject of the murder. She needn't have worried. Apparently Tim was only too eager to discuss it—a trait that had landed him in trouble with the police chief more than once.

"Too bad someone had to ruin it," he said, slipping his wallet into his jacket pocket. "I hope the murder won't make people too anxious to go to the fairgrounds. If the rodeo doesn't do well they won't be back, and that would be a bummer."

"So you're a big rodeo fan, then?"

"Yeah. Saw a lot of them when I was out West." He took the bagged book from her. "Guess I'll be seeing a lot of this one. Dan and I have been questioning everyone, though I'm pretty sure we've got the perp."

Clara's spirits sank. "You've got proof?"

Tim grinned. "I keep forgetting you're an amateur detective."

"Not really. Just interested in the law and how it works, that's all."

"That's not what Dan calls it. He calls it interfering with the law. You have to admit, you do seem to get involved with our local murder investigations."

"Dumb luck, I guess." She met his gaze squarely. "So you've arrested Lisa Warren's killer, then?"

Tim sighed. "All right, I'll tell you what I know, but only if you swear you won't start running around questioning people."

Clara faked a look of hurt innocence. "Why would I do that if you've already arrested the killer?"

Tim glanced over his shoulder, then, apparently satisfied, leaned over the counter. "We haven't actually arrested him yet, but it's only a matter of time. One of the barrel racers at the rodeo saw the victim heading toward the concert stage around eight fifteen. Our guy is a calf roper, but I figure you already know that, seeing as how he's a friend of Rick's and you've met him. Anyway, he was last seen in the stands about that time. No one saw him after that until he turned up at the chutes around ten minutes to nine. He said he was talking to fans, but no one can verify that."

Clara frowned. "It doesn't sound like much to go on. As a matter of fact, I was talking to Wes around eight. He gave us free tickets for the show."

"Yeah, I know. Rick told me. That still would have given Carlton plenty of time to get down to the stage and kill Lisa Warren. It was his rope that was wrapped around the victim's neck, and it was no secret that he had the hots for her. Dan figures Lisa gave him the brush-off and he turned nasty. Some of these rodeo boys can be pretty hotheaded."

"Hi, Tim! You talking about the rodeo?"

Tim turned his head as Molly came up behind him. Looking sheepish, he murmured, "Just chatting. Have you seen it yet?"

"No, I'm going tonight." Molly dumped a pile of books on the counter. "I can't wait. It should be a blast."

"Well, guess I should be going." Tim headed for the door. "Stay out of trouble."

Molly frowned as the door closed behind him. "Was he talking to you or me?"

"Both of us, I guess." Clara pointed at the books. "What are they?"

Molly grinned. "Books."

"I can see that. Why are they on the counter?"

"I can't figure out if they should go in the sci-fi section or the fantasy section."

Clara picked up one of the books. "Sometimes it's hard to tell. It helps if you remember that sci-fi is based on science and technology, and is usually related to what's real, while fantasy is imaginary and related to stuff that doesn't exist."

"Wow." Molly looked impressed. "That's major." She chose another book from the pile. "I guess I should read the back blurbs."

"Well, usually either Stephanie or I stock the shelves, so you haven't had much practice. If you do it often enough, after a while you'll be able to spot which is which." Clara placed the book back on the pile. "If in doubt, you can always check the reviews online."

"Thanks, I'll do that." Molly gave her a sly glance. "So are you and Stephanie going to investigate the rodeo murder?"

"No, we're not." Clara moved over to the computer. "This is one crime Dan will have to solve on his own."

"Too bad. It was fun helping you guys." Molly picked up the books. "Guess I'll take these down to the Reading Nook and try to figure out where they go."

"Okay, but keep an eye out for customers. I have to check the stockroom to see what we need for the high school's required reading. Let me know if you need help."

"Will do!" Molly sailed out of sight.

Alone in the stockroom, Clara tried not to think about the murder. Dwelling on crimes tended to trigger a vision, and she'd had enough of those in the past two days. It was up to Dan now to find out if Rick's buddy was involved.

Thinking about Rick was much more pleasant. As if she'd conjured him up, Molly opened the stockroom door a short time later and announced, "This is one customer you'll want to take care of yourself."

Rick appeared behind Molly, peering over her shoulder. "There you are. I thought you might have gone home." He edged around her and stepped inside.

"Not until closing time." Clara nodded at Molly, who closed the door with a lewd wink. "Did you need something?"

"Just wanted to talk." He glanced around at the boxes, packages and piles of books. "Looks like you'll be keeping busy. Does all this stuff have to go out on the shelves?"

"Not all of it. Some of it is returns. They have to be stripped and the covers sent back for refunds."

"Ouch." He winced. "Destroying books seems like such a sacrilege."

"I know what you mean." She studied his face. "You didn't come here to discuss books, though."

"No, I didn't." He stuck his hands in his pants pockets. "Dan let Wes go."

"Oh, I'm so glad." She hesitated, knowing from his expression that all was not well. "He's cleared him?"

"Not exactly." He sighed. "They don't have enough

evidence to hold him, that's all. Which means he's still under suspicion. As you know, I've been there and I know only too well what that's like. All those weird looks from people you thought were your friends. The feeling that nobody trusts you, or worse, that they're afraid of you." His shoulders slumped. "Wes said that even the guys in the rodeo are avoiding him. This could end his career."

Clara briefly laid a hand on his arm. "I'm sorry, Rick. I know you're worried about him. Like I said, if he's innocent, the truth will come out eventually."

"I know he didn't do it." He placed his hands on her shoulders. "I hate to ask this, because it could mean trouble for you, but I don't know what else to do."

"You want me to ask questions."

His mouth twitched in a wry smile. "You do seem to have a way of finding out stuff. People talk to you and tell you things they wouldn't tell a cop. I'm not asking you to track down the killer. I don't want you putting yourself in danger again. I just want to know the answer to a couple of questions, that's all. Then maybe I can take it from there."

"Like what?"

"Anita Beaumont. She's a barrel racer. From what Wes told me, she knows more about Lisa than anyone. She didn't have much to say to Tim when he questioned her, but maybe she'll open up to another woman."

Clara hesitated. Her vision of a man in a red shirt standing over Lisa's body was still fresh in her mind.

What if she asked questions and got answers that incriminated Wes even further?

The anguish in Rick's eyes, however, was too painful to ignore. "All right. What do you want me to ask her?"

Rick pulled her into his arms for a quick hug, then let her go. "Thank you. Just promise me you won't go chasing after clues and stuff."

"Don't worry. I won't."

"Good. Anita might know why Lisa went to the concert stage in the first place. She must have been meeting someone there. Wes swears it wasn't him. So we need to know who it was."

"Okay, I'll ask."

"See if you can find out who else was interested in Lisa. According to Tim, she was pretty hot stuff. Wes wasn't the only one who was chasing her."

"So Wes really was attracted to her?"

"Yeah." Rick looked uncomfortable. "He's pretty broken up about the whole thing. It's bad enough that he had to lose her that way, but to be accused of killing her is just about destroying him."

"I'll do what I can." Right then she would have done anything to take away the misery on his face. "Where can I find Anita?"

"She shares a trailer with another contestant, Melosa Sanchez. They're parked in a field behind the fairgrounds. If you go over there in the morning you should be able to find her around somewhere. I'll come with you if you like, but I figure she'll talk more freely without me looking over your shoulder."

"It's okay. I'll take Stephanie with me." Clara crossed her fingers that her cousin would go along. "She's good at getting women to talk."

"Thanks." He pulled her close again. "Just be careful, okay?"

"Don't worry. I'll take Tatters along, too. He'll protect us."

"Now I feel better." He grinned. "How's the monster doing, anyway? Still keeping your mom on her toes?"

"That goes for both of us." She tilted her head to one side. "Did you hear that?"

Rick lifted his chin. "Hear what?"

"I'm not sure." She listened for a moment, then shook her head. "I might be imagining things, but I keep thinking I hear a noise. A sort of scuffling sound. But when I listen for it, I can never hear it."

"Could be a mouse. Or a rat."

Clara shivered. "Don't think the thought hasn't crossed my mind."

"You might want to get an exterminator in here."

"I'll talk to Stephanie about it. I—" A loud rapping on the door interrupted her.

Molly's muffled voice declared, "I need help!"

"Gotta go." Clara darted to the door. "I'll let you know what happens tomorrow."

He followed her out, then waved good-bye as he went out the front door.

Clara was busy with customers for the rest of the day, and by the time she was ready to close up, her feet ached and all she could think about was getting home. Not that she'd get to rest, since Tatters would be dancing on toenails waiting to go for his walk. First, however, she had to eat something. Her stomach felt like a deflated balloon.

Jessie wasn't home, and had left a note with a reminder that she was at her book club. She'd also left a salad in the fridge, and Clara sat down to enjoy it, with Tatters lying at her feet, ears twitching with every sound she made.

When she stood up to take her plate to the sink, he sat up. *About time. Now we walk.*

"Yes, your majesty. Just as soon as I've cleaned up here."

Tatters stood, yawned, then strolled out of the kitchen.

Shaking her head, Clara rinsed her plate and placed it in the dishwasher. Stopping by the fridge, she grabbed a bottle of water and took it out into the living room. The dog had disappeared—he was probably waiting for her at the front door.

She grabbed the leash and her light jacket and walked out into the hallway. Sure enough, Tatters sat by the front door, muscles tensed to spring the minute she opened it. "Let's go, buddy," she said, as she fastened the leash to the dog's collar. "I have to talk to Stephanie when we get back." Tomorrow she faced the task of questioning a woman who so far had been uncooperative. She needed Stephanie by her side.

Anxious to talk to her cousin, she cut Tatters' run on the beach shorter than usual, much to his disgust. He showed his displeasure by dragging on the leash all the way home, stopping continually to sniff at tree trunks, poles, water hydrants and anything else that looked vaguely interesting.

Finally losing her patience, Clara yelled at him, "Quit this right now! Either you keep moving or there's no bed-time treat."

Tatters sniffed, stuck his nose in the air and set off at a pace that kept her running the rest of the way.

Once inside the house, she unhooked his leash and, breathing hard, headed for her bedroom. He followed close behind her and jumped up on the bed, scrabbling at the comforter to find the perfect spot. Ignoring him, she sat on the edge and tapped Stephanie's number on her cell phone.

Her cousin answered on the second ring. "Good timing. I just got the kids to bed. We can actually talk without interruption."

Clara smiled. "That'll make a change." Most of her conversations with Stephanie were punctuated by her cousin yelling at one of her three kids or begging her husband to take care of them. George had little control over his two youngest, who were as wild and unpredict-able as their mother had been when she was their age.

"So tell me how the date went with Rick. Did he kiss you good-night?"

"He did, as a matter of fact, though it's none of your business."

This went right over Stephanie's head. "Was it a long, romantic kiss, or just a quick peck on the lips?"

Clara sighed. "If you must know, it was short and sweet. We were both shaken up by the murder and in no mood for any romantic stuff."

"Oh, phooey. I was hoping for all the juicy details."

"Even if there had been juicy details, I wouldn't be telling you about them. There are some things that are sacred."

"But—"

"Speaking of the murder, I have a favor to ask you."

To Clara's relief, her cousin abandoned her inquisition. Her voice brightened considerably when she answered, "Are we going to hunt down another killer?"

"No!" Clara softened her tone. "At least, not directly. Rick just wants me to talk to one of the barrel racers tomorrow morning. I thought you might like to come along. That's if Molly doesn't mind holding down the fort again."

"She won't mind. We shouldn't be that busy." Stephanie's voice changed. "I don't understand. Why does Rick want you to talk to a barrel racer?"

Clara hesitated, then decided the news would probably be out by tomorrow. "Dan took Wes Carlton in for questioning today."

"Wes who?"

"Carlton. Rick's buddy in the rodeo."

"Oh, wow. I bet Rick's upset about that."

"He is. They released Wes, but until the killer is caught, people are bound to think Wes is guilty. Rick's afraid it will ruin Wes's career."

"Why did they arrest him in the first place?"

"Apparently he had an argument with the woman earlier that afternoon, he doesn't have an alibi for the time of the murder and it was his pigging string that was used to strangle her."

"Hmm." Stephanie paused, then added, "What the heck's a picking string?"

"Pigging." Clara spelled it out. "The contestants use it to tie down the calves."

"Poor things." Again the long pause. "Are you sure this Wes guy didn't do it?"

"Nope. But Rick is, and I respect his judgment."

"Well, I hope he's right, 'cos I'd hate to get involved and have Dan come down hard on us like he always does and then we find out the guy is guilty after all. That would really take a spoke out of Dan's wheel. He'd probably throw us in jail."

"That's a chance we'll have to take." Clara hesitated before adding, "Or I will. I'll understand if you'd rather stay out of this one."

"Are you kidding? And let you go off into the valley of death without me? No way, cuz. I'm in, for good or bad. Like always."

Clara smiled. "Thanks. I really don't want to do this without you."

"You won't have to. So Rick wants us to ask questions at the rodeo? I've been wondering what it's like. The rodeo, I mean. I tried to talk George into taking me, but he's not the least bit interested. He said I should go with you, but you've already seen it, and I don't know anyone else I'd want to go with."

"Well, you can go backstage with me tomorrow morning. That's the next best thing."

"Can't wait." Stephanie mumbled something under her breath. "I can hear Michael and Olivia arguing. Gotta go. What time tomorrow?"

"I'll pick you up at the bookstore. Around ten? That'll give us a couple of hours before I have to start my shift."

"Sounds good."

Stephanie clicked off, and Clara laid the phone on her bedside table. Glancing at Tatters, she saw the intent look in his eyes. "Yes, you're going, too."

The sound of the front door opening turned both their heads. Clara got up from the bed. "Come on, boy. Let's say good-night to Mom." Then, she promised herself, she'd get some sleep. Tomorrow promised to be an interesting day.

4

Stephanie was behind the counter when Clara arrived at the bookstore the next morning. Her cousin was scrabbling through a drawer, shaking her head and muttering to herself.

"What are you looking for?" Clara leaned across the counter. "Can I help?"

"I don't think so." Stephanie shut the drawer with an exasperated sigh. "John Halloran was in here a while ago. He swears he put in an order for the Knights of Wisdom series, but it's not in the computer. He said he wrote it down and gave it to me, but I can't find it anywhere." She looked at Clara, her face a picture of misery. "Am I getting senile?"

Clara smiled. "Of course not. You're just a very busy wife, mother and bookstore owner. You work most mornings, and the rest of the time you're chasing around after that family of yours. No wonder things get misplaced."

Stephanie shook her head. "I used to manage better than this."

"You probably need a vacation." Clara looked around. The cookbooks were neatly displayed on their table, the end displays were full of the latest releases, the stand next to the door held an assortment of postcards, bookmarks and calendars and the smell of coffee wafted up from the Reading Nook. "It looks like everything here is under control. Is Molly around?"

"I'll call her." Stephanie rang the bell on the counter and a moment later Molly appeared from the aisles.

She bounded forward when she saw Clara. "There you are. I never got to see the rodeo after all. Dan shut down last night's show because of the murder investigation. Have you heard anything more about it?"

"Not yet." Clara sent her cousin a warning glance. "I'm sorry you didn't get to see the rodeo."

Molly shrugged. "No prob. They're putting on an extra show on Monday afternoon for everyone who missed it last night. That way they can keep up with the events schedule."

"Great. Then you'll see it after all."

"Yeah. So where are you two off to?"

Clara tried to sound casual. "We have to take care of a couple of things. I hope you don't mind being on your own for an hour or two?"

Molly grinned. "No, I like it. Gives me a feeling of power."

"Come on then, Steffie." Clara headed for the door.

"Are you two investigating the murder?"

Clara briefly closed her eyes. She might have known she couldn't keep it a secret from Molly. "Not investigating exactly. Just asking questions."

"Cool." Molly's eyes glistened with excitement. "Let me know if I can help."

"Will do. Thanks!" Clara tilted her head toward the door, signaling her cousin to get a move on.

Stephanie grabbed her purse and joined Clara at the door. "I'll have my cell on, so call me if you need help with anything."

"I'll be fine." Molly looked wistful. "Go have fun out there."

"We'll try." Stephanie sailed out the door behind her cousin.

Together they hurried down the hill to the parking lot, where Clara had left her car. Already the sun warmed the sidewalks, and just a couple of fluffy white clouds dotted the sky. Between the buildings at the end of the street she could see the wide expanse of blue-green water. Here and there a yacht glided gracefully across the waves, and in the distance a cargo ship chugged along the horizon.

Clara pulled off her jacket and slung it over her arm. "I hope we can find this Anita person. Rick says she's staying in a trailer in a field behind the fairgrounds, but if she's not there when we get there I guess we'll have to look for her."

"Shouldn't be a problem, should it?" They'd reached the car, and Stephanie pulled open the passenger door.

"I don't know if they'll let us wander around the place."

"We could always pretend we're groupies looking for autographs."

Clara pulled a face. "I can't imagine that'll get us far." She climbed in and closed the door. "We could say we're friends of Wes, I guess."

"If he's under suspicion for murder, that's probably not going to help much."

"Woof!" Tatters said in agreement from the backseat.

Stephanie uttered a little shriek. "You didn't tell me you were bringing the monster."

Hey! Tatters stuck his nose into her neck, making her shriek again.

Clara gave him a stern look. "Behave."

Tatters grumbled deep in his throat.

Clara scowled, and the dog sat back on the seat.

"So much for my allergies," Stephanie said, slumping her shoulders.

"You keep saying that, and I keep telling you, you don't have allergies."

"Well, my kids do."

"They're not here."

"No, but I'll be taking dog hairs in with me."

Clara started the engine, turning on the air conditioner

so that cool air filtered throughout the car. "You always said you felt safer with Tatters along."

Yeah, so how about that, Miss Fusspot?

Clara gave him another reproving glance.

"I do, I guess. I just wish he wouldn't shed hairs all over me."

"Well, let's hope we won't need him and he can stay in the car." Clara nosed the car into the street and took off down the rest of the hill.

Mercifully, Tatters was quiet as they drove along the coast road. Gazing at the heaving water, Clara wished she were walking along the beach instead of heading into another murder investigation.

She was doing this for Rick, she reminded herself, as they reached the fairgrounds and followed the gravel road into the field behind.

The rides and booths had been set up across from the stadium, and people strolled around, most hanging onto kids bouncing along with excitement. Shrieks and screams erupted from the roller coaster and the parachute ride, almost drowned out by the music blaring from the bumper cars and carousel.

Clara parked the car and turned to Tatters, who was watching the scene with intense concentration. "Stay," she said firmly. "We won't be long."

The dog looked at her with soulful eyes. *Why can't I go with you?*

"Not now."

Stephanie stared at her. "Not now what?"

Clara hastily wound down all four windows. "Nothing. I was just talking to myself."

"The first signs of senility." Stephanie climbed out of the car and shut the door. "You do that a lot," she added when Clara had joined her.

"Do what?"

"Talk to yourself. Especially when you're with that dog." Stephanie's eyes narrowed. "Or maybe you're talking to the dog, like he's human or something."

"Everyone talks to their dogs like they're humans. If you had one, you'd know."

"I have a cat. I don't think he's human."

"Cats are different." Clara nudged her cousin's arm. "Let's go find those trailers."

Passing by the rides, she could now see the trailers dotting the grass at the far end of the field. A couple of cowboys sat on the steps of an RV, and a young woman led a horse over to a corral where several other horses were grazing. Another woman followed her with two black labs trotting at her side.

Clara led her cousin over to the RV, where the cowboys were in deep conversation. Pausing in front of them, she said brightly, "Excuse me! Could you tell me where I can find Anita Beaumont?"

Both heads turned in her direction and studied her in silence for so long, Clara began to feel uncomfortable.

Finally one of them drawled, "You the law?"

"Oh no." Clara glanced at her cousin for help but Stephanie was gazing at the men as if she'd never seen a cowboy before. "We . . . er . . . just want to talk to her, that's all. We're friends of Wes Carlton."

The men's expressions changed, and she wished she hadn't mentioned Wes's name.

One of the men jerked his thumb in the direction of the corral. "Anita's over there. She's the redhead."

Clara followed the direction of his thumb. The woman had reached the corral and was herding her horse through the gate. The sun gleamed on her long, auburn hair. The woman behind her was dark-haired and taller, and she paused at the fence while the dogs wandered off to sniff at the grass.

"Thanks." Clara grabbed Stephanie's arm and headed for the corral.

As they stepped over power cables and water hoses, the strains of a country song from someone's radio followed them.

"Good thing you left Tatters in the car," Stephanie said, nodding at the two dogs. "He could have started a riot with those two." She sniffed the air. "I can smell bacon."

"And coffee. Just as well we already had breakfast."

"I'm still hungry."

"You'll have to wait for lunch."

The two rodeo women were inside the corral now, watching the horses. Clara slowed her step. She wished now she'd rehearsed her speech. How do you go about asking a woman if her dead friend was having an affair?

Reaching the fence, she muttered, "I'll do the talking. You jump in if things get awkward."

"What else?" Stephanie waved at the women, who had turned to look at them. "Hi, there! Nice horses."

The two women glanced at each other, but neither answered Stephanie's greeting.

"This is going to be fun," Clara muttered to Stephanie as she forced a smile. "We're friends of Wes Carlton," she called out. "Could we have a word with you?"

Anita said something to the other woman, then walked slowly toward the fence. Her freckled face was taut with suspicion, and her full lips were clamped so tightly together Clara doubted she'd ever get a word out of her.

Anita Beaumont had the strong, slender build of an athlete, though that heavy mop of red hair made her look more like a shampoo model. The wariness in her hazel eyes betrayed her uneasiness, and she paused in front of the cousins, waiting in silence for them to speak.

Clara decided to take the soft approach. "I'm so sorry for your loss. I know Lisa Warren was a good friend. It must be hard, going on with the show without her."

Confusion flashed in Anita's eyes. "Who said she was my friend?"

Clara stumbled over her words. "Er . . . Wes did. I think."

Anita's thin brows drew together. "Wes said that?" She

shook her head. "I knew her, sure. Most of us regulars on the circuit knew Lisa. She was with the rodeo for years before she went to work for Paul Eastcott. She's no friend of mine, though, and Wes knows it." Her expression changed to one of guilt. "Of course I'm sorry she's dead. No one deserves to die that way."

"Exactly." Clara smiled. "We've been wondering who could have possibly done this terrible thing."

Anita's frown deepened. "Did you know Lisa?"

Clara hesitated and Stephanie answered for her. "No, but we know Wes, and we don't think he was capable of killing anyone."

"So what exactly do you want from me?"

"Just some answers." Clara leaned an elbow on the fence in an effort to look nonchalant. "Like if anyone else might have had a reason to get rid of Lisa."

Anita's chin came up. "Okay, that's it. Just because I used to be jealous of Lisa doesn't mean I killed her. I know the cops found that e-mail I sent her, threatening her if she didn't stay away from Wes, but that was months ago, when Lisa was still on the circuit and long before she moved to Mittleford. Besides, I have an alibi. The cops already cleared me, and I don't talk to reporters, so you can just take your questions and—"

"Whoa, wait a minute." Clara held up her hand. "We're not accusing you of anything. And we're not cops or reporters. We're just good friends of Wes who don't want to see him go to jail for something he didn't do."

"She's right," Stephanie put in. She briefly laid a hand on Anita's arm. "If you care at all about Wes, you'll help us find out who did this."

Anita stared at her from under thick, dark, mascaraed lashes. "Who exactly are you?"

"We told you," Clara said, giving Stephanie a grateful nod. "We know the police chief and he's convinced Wes is guilty. We'd like to show him how wrong he is about all this."

Now Anita looked worried. "But the cops let Wes go."

"It doesn't mean they won't arrest him later. They're trying to dig up more evidence against him right now."

"Well, they won't get anything out of me."

Clara sighed. It was beginning to look as if she wouldn't get anything out of Anita, either. She could tell the woman was hiding something. The Sense voice was buzzing loud and clear in her ear.

There had been a time or two when she'd been able to read someone's mind, but it was rare. Most of the time, if someone really didn't want anyone to know what he was thinking, it wasn't that hard to block his thoughts. All she could tell was that Anita knew something important and wasn't willing to share it.

"That's great," Stephanie said, "but the police are very good at making mountains out of molehills. Wes could be in a lot of trouble while he's trying to prove his innocence, and all the bad publicity could ruin his career. You might never see him again after all this is over."

Anita's eyebrows shot up. "You really think so?

Stephanie solemnly nodded. "I do."

Anita stared down at her bright blue cowboy boots for several seconds, then reluctantly lifted her head. "All right, I'll tell you what I know. Only if you swear on God's green earth that you won't tell a soul that I told you."

"You have our sacred promise," Clara assured her.

"All right. The last time I saw Lisa, it was right around eight fifteen that night. I know that because we'd just gotten through with our event. Melosa and I were walking away from the arena to get ice cream and we saw Lisa heading toward the concert stage. I could tell by the way she was hurrying and looking around that she was afraid of being seen. I think she was going to meet someone and wanted to keep it a secret."

"And could that have been Wes?"

Anger flared in Anita's eyes. "No, it couldn't. I know he had a major crush on her, but she didn't want anything to do with him. In fact, she was mean to him. She told him once that he had no manners and he smelled bad. There's no way she'd sneak out to meet him anywhere. If she was meeting someone, it wasn't Wes Carlton."

The woman's thought came through loud and clear in Clara's head. "But you think you know who it might have been."

Again Anita hesitated, then slowly nodded her head. "You might want to talk to Paul Eastcott. He's the production manager at the Hill Top Resort, and he's in charge of the rodeo. Lisa was his assistant. She told me they were in love and that she was going to marry Paul. She said he was going to ask his wife for a divorce." Anita uttered a scornful laugh. "Like that was going to happen. Diane has it all—looks, money—her family owns the Hill Top chain. She was responsible for the new resort being built here. She likes living here and she's hoping Paul won't travel so much now there's a Hill Top in Finn's Harbor. Paul's living the good life right now, and he'd never have given up all that for Lisa. If he really was having an affair with her, he was just playing with her."

Clara exchanged a meaningful look with her cousin. "Do you know where we can find him?"

Anita glanced at her watch. "He's either at home or in his office at the resort. I did hear he was interviewing for another assistant, so I'd try the office first."

"Thank you, Anita. You've been really helpful."

"You're welcome." Anita grabbed her arm. "You swear you won't tell him or anyone else what I told you? If word gets around that I bad-mouthed Paul, he might find a way to get back at me."

"I swear."

"Me, too," Stephanie promised.

Anita's fingers tightened on Clara's arm. "You really think you can help Wes?"

"I hope so." Clara smiled as the woman let go of her arm. "We'll certainly do our best to clear his name." She started to leave, then turned back. "Oh, by the way, do you happen to own a red shirt?"

Anita's laugh sounded forced. "No way. Can you imagine how that would clash with my hair?"

"Oh, right." Clara turned away again, while the voice in her head said over and over again, *She's lying. She's lying. She's lying.*

———

"So what was that red shirt thing all about?" Stephanie demanded as they walked back to the car.

"It was in one of my visions. I saw someone standing over Lisa's body, and he was wearing a red shirt. It just occurred to me I only saw the back of him. It could have been a woman."

"You think Anita killed Lisa?"

"Maybe. She had a motive. She's obviously fond of Wes, and he was chasing after Lisa. Maybe she figured if she got rid of Lisa, she'd have more of a chance with him."

Stephanie looked back at the corral, where Anita was talking to the other woman. "She looks tough enough to have done it, but if she's in love with Wes, why would she try to pin the murder on him?"

"She might not have intended to implicate him. She could have just happened to have his rope with her when she met with Lisa. Maybe they argued, and it got out of control."

"I don't know." Stephanie looked doubtful. "She just

doesn't seem like the murdering type." Clara smiled. "You know what they say about a woman scorned. And, as you already pointed out, she's definitely tough enough to have done it. On the other hand, she said she didn't have a red shirt. If she's telling the truth about that, she's not the person in my vision."

"I wonder if Wes has a red shirt."

Clara reluctantly nodded. "He does. He was wearing it at the rodeo."

"Oh crap."

"He can't be the only one who owns a red shirt."

"No, of course not." Stephanie brightened her voice. "All we have to do is find out who else has one."

"And the proof to go with it. Nobody's going to listen to me rambling on about my visions."

Stephanie made a face. "You're right about that." She climbed into the car and slammed the door. "So where are we going now?"

"To talk to Paul Eastcott."

"He's not going to admit to you or anyone else that he was having an affair with a murdered woman."

"Maybe not, but I've wanted to get a look at the new resort ever since it opened. This is a good excuse to get inside and check the place out."

Behind her, Tatters yawned. *I gotta pee.*

Clara sighed and opened her door again. "I'd better take Tatters for a quick walk. Do you want to come, or would you rather wait here for us?"

"I'll wait here." Stephanie fished her cell phone out of her purse. "I need to call Molly and see how things are going at the store."

Leaving her cousin to make her call, Clara fastened Tatters' leash and led him across the grass to the trees. The raucous sounds of the carnival faded as they followed a rough trail into the woods, until finally Tatters found the right spot to lift his leg.

They had just started back when the dog uttered a low growl and stopped, a tuft of hair rising on the back of his neck.

Startled, Clara peered up the trail and was surprised to see how far they had wandered. "What is it, boy?"

Tatters answered with another growl.

She could hear it now—the snapping of twigs as someone blundered through the trees somewhere on her right. There was something ominous in the sound, and she waited, holding tightly to Tatters' leash, as whoever it was drew closer.

5

Tatters stood in fighting mode, feet planted firmly, ears pointed forward, hackles rising.

Clara felt a strong urge to run, and in the next instant chided herself for being so paranoid. Even so, she surged ahead, tugging on Tatters' leash when he showed no signs of wanting to follow her.

"Come on, boy," she said, giving him another tug. "Steffie's waiting for us."

Tatters growled again and this time leapt past her to stand in front of her. As he did so, a man stepped out from behind some shrubbery, making every nerve in Clara's body spring to attention.

At first she didn't recognize him, and fear formed a

lump in her throat as he limped toward her, a grin widening his mouth.

"Clara, isn't it? I thought I recognized that voice."

The soft tone was familiar, and she frowned.

The man tilted his cowboy hat with his thumb. "Guess you don't know me without my makeup."

Clara's brow cleared. Of course. Marty Pearce. He looked totally different from when she'd last seen him. He was older and thinner than she'd thought, with deep lines cutting into his forehead and at the corners of his eyes. His face looked drawn, but the dark eyes smiling at her were the eyes of the clown.

Letting out her breath in one big puff, Clara gave him a weak smile. "Hi, Marty." Tatters was still bristling in front of her, and she gave a warning tug on his leash. "I was just taking my dog for a walk."

"That's one handsome dog." Marty grinned at Tatters but made no move to approach him. "I thought I heard someone out here. I take a walk every morning to loosen up the muscles." He waved a hand at the fairgrounds. "It's not easy to get away from all that hubbub going on over there. It's nice to find peace and quiet for a little while." He tipped his head to one side. "So what are you doing out here, hon? Planning on joining the rodeo?"

Clara laughed, beginning to feel more at ease. "I don't think I'd do very well. I've never been on the back of a horse."

His eyes lit up. "No kidding. You don't know what

you're missing. It would sure be a pleasure to give you a lesson or two."

"Thanks, but I think I'll pass. I'm not really into horses."

"Well, if you change your mind, you know where to find me."

Clara hesitated. Now was her chance to warn the clown of possible danger—but how to do it without sounding like a complete idiot? She began cautiously, trying to sound unconcerned. "I was so sorry to hear about the murder of Lisa Warren. That must have been such a shock to everyone."

Marty's smile vanished. "Yeah. She was a great gal. We'll all miss her."

"You knew her well, then?"

"Most of us regulars knew Lisa. She traveled on the circuit for a few years. Then she met Paul Eastcott. He sets up rodeos all over the country for the Hill Top chain. He was looking for an assistant, and Lisa took the job."

He shook his head and continued. "What a waste. Bad for business, too. We were shut down last night, and who knows if we'll make that up. People are gonna think twice about going someplace where someone's just been murdered."

"Well, perhaps the police will catch the killer and put everyone's mind at rest."

"Yeah. I couldn't believe the cops arrested Wes. He's got a bit of a temper, but murder?" He lifted his shoulders. "Just goes to show you can never really know people."

Clara frowned. "The police let Wes go."

Marty nodded. "Lack of evidence, so I heard. They're still asking questions about him, though, so I guess they haven't ruled him out."

"Do you think he killed Lisa?"

Again the shrug. "Who knows? It could have been anyone, I guess. But the murder weapon belonged to Wes, and everyone knows he was chasing after Lisa." His eyes hardened. "Lisa was always real blunt about the way she felt about people. Maybe she upset him once too often."

Clara was about to answer when a cold wind seemed to blow up from nowhere. One minute she was standing on a woodland trail and the next she was in the darkened parking lot again. A pickup truck barreled toward her, barely missing her as it roared past. When the dust cleared she could see the clown lying on the ground, his black and white costume smeared in blood.

She cried out loud, and the scene vanished. Tatters whined, and she looked down to see the dog staring up at her.

"Are you okay?" Marty was staring at her too, concern written all over his face.

She patted her stomach. "Just a bout of indigestion. Guess I'd better get something to eat."

Marty looked relieved. "I'll walk with you if it's okay with your guard dog."

Clara laughed, though she didn't feel at all amused. "Tatters is a sweetheart when you get to know him."

The clown glanced down at the dog but still kept his distance. "I'll take your word for it. I got bitten once, and ever since then I've been real careful around dogs."

"Oh, I'm sorry." Clara paused a moment, then added, "I guess there are all kinds of danger in your job."

"Danger?" He seemed taken aback by the suggestion. "It used to be dangerous when I was messing with the bulls, I guess, but I don't do that anymore. I let one of the brutes get the better of me." He patted his knee. "That's how I got this bum leg. Had to replace the knee joint, but the shin bone got pretty messed up. It never did heal right. I can't run anymore, so fighting bulls is out for me."

"I'm so sorry." She felt genuine pity for the man. It must have been hard for him to lose his career like that. "But you must enjoy entertaining the crowds. Especially the kids. They adore you."

His smile brightened his whole face. "When I hear those little kids' laughter, it makes up for everything. I can feel their love while I'm out there." He gave her a knowing wink. "Everyone needs love in their lives, right, hon?"

"Right." She was feeling frustrated. Somehow she had to warn him. Maybe she should just come out and say it. "Still, with all that tumbling around that you do, you must worry about getting hurt again."

He shrugged again. "What's a few bruises here and there, when you can make a little kid happy?"

"Just be careful, okay?"

He gave her a startled look. "Don't you worry. I will."

"I'd hate to see something really bad happen to you."

Now he was frowning. "Are you trying to tell me something?"

She felt awkward, aware that she was getting into deep water. "It's just intuition. What you do seems dangerous to me and I just don't want you to get hurt."

His frown disappeared. "You're a sweet lady, hon. That young man of yours is real lucky. You can tell him that from me."

She laughed. "Thanks. Maybe I will." She had done her best, she assured herself. There wasn't much more she could say without sounding paranoid.

They had reached the clearing where Stephanie waited in the car. Glancing over at the group of trailers, Clara noticed a handful of pickup trucks alongside. She wished she'd been able to see more clearly the truck in her vision. It had been too dark to see what color it was, or make out any distinguishable marks on it.

"I hope the show goes well tonight," she said, as Tatters strained on the leash.

"It should, considering everyone had a night's rest. I just hope we get the crowds in to watch it." He lifted his hand in a salute. "Thanks for the company. I enjoyed talking to you."

"You, too." She watched him limp off, while Tatters pulled impatiently on the leash again.

The sound of her car's horn made her jump. Opening

the rear door, she waited for the dog to jump into the backseat.

Stephanie twisted around in her seat to glare at her. "You sure took your sweet time. How far does that dog need to go to pee?"

"Sorry. I was talking to Marty."

"That was the clown?" Stephanie peered through the windshield at the figure disappearing into the crowd. "He sure doesn't look all that creepy. I would have liked to meet him."

"Maybe another time." Clara started the engine. "Right now we have to get up to the resort and talk to Paul Eastcott if I'm to make it back to the bookstore in time for my shift. How is Molly doing, anyway?"

"She's okay. She says it's pretty quiet for a Friday."

Noticing her cousin's frown, Clara nudged her arm. "Cheer up. By this afternoon the shop will be full of tourists."

"From your mouth to God's ear."

Clara shifted the gear stick and took her foot off the brake. The next instant she slammed the brake down again as a figure appeared in front of her.

Recognizing Anita's companion from the corral, Clara shut off the engine and rolled down her window.

"I'm Melosa," the woman said, peering through the window with a worried frown. "I just wanted a quick word with you."

"Sure." Clara waited, but Melosa backed away, making it obvious she wanted her to get out of the car.

Clara opened the door. "I won't be a minute," she muttered, and stepped out.

Melosa backed up another step or two, looking as if she might turn tail and run any minute. "I—I heard you talking to Anita, and . . ." She glanced at the car, then lowered her voice. "I don't want to get anyone into trouble, but . . ." Her words trailed off and she clutched her throat.

"It's okay," Clara said, feeling sorry for the woman. It was obvious she was upset about something. "No one's going to get into trouble without good reason. What did you want to tell me?"

Melosa looked over her shoulder. "Promise me you won't tell Anita I talked to you?"

Clara held up her hand. "I swear."

The woman lowered her voice even more. "I wasn't with her when she said she saw Lisa. She made me tell the police that, so she'd have an alibi. She said we'd both need an alibi or we'd be suspects in the murder. I was frightened what she might do if I didn't say what she wanted, but now I'm scared the cops will find out I lied and arrest me."

Clara smiled. "I don't think they'll do that if you tell them what you told me."

Melosa shook her head so violently her long, black hair swished in front of her face. Brushing the heavy strands aside, she muttered, "I can't talk to the police. That's why I'm telling *you*. I just felt I had to tell someone, and when

I heard you talking to Anita about Lisa, I thought you should know. Please don't tell the cops what I told you."

"All right." Clara opened the car door again. "Try not to worry. I'm sure the police will find out who killed Lisa and then all this will be over."

Melosa stepped closer. "I hope it wasn't Wes. It would break Anita's heart. She's loco about him—even though he had eyes for no one but Lisa. Anita even stole things that belonged to him. She said it made her feel closer to him. I saw a glove, a belt, a shirt—"

Clara straightened. "A red shirt?"

Melosa's eyes widened. "Yes, it was. How do you know?"

Clara shrugged. "Just a guess. I don't suppose you saw her with his pigging string?"

Sheer horror flooded the other woman's face. "You don't think Anita killed Lisa? She wouldn't . . . she couldn't . . . I shouldn't have said anything. Please forget what I told you."

Clara hurried to reassure her. "I'm not thinking anything, Melosa. Just asking, that's all. Don't worry. I won't be talking to the police."

"Thank you." Looking unconvinced, Melosa hurried off.

"So what was that all about?" Stephanie asked, as Clara slid onto her seat. "I couldn't hear what she was saying."

Starting the engine again, Clara repeated what Melosa had told her. "I think she's really scared, though I'm not sure why. I told her I wouldn't tell anyone what she said, but I can't promise to keep quiet about this if the police ask questions."

"Well, you know how Dan feels about us 'interfering in police business,' as he calls it." Stephanie fastened her seat belt. "It will be better for us if he doesn't know we talked to anyone about the murder."

"I couldn't agree more. Somehow he always finds out, though."

"Well let's hope he doesn't find out this time, or we'll be in deep trouble." She looked at her watch. "Let's go. I'm getting hungrier by the minute."

"You're always hungry." Clara drove out of the field and headed back to the coast road. "I don't know why you don't carry snacks with you."

Yeah! Tatters nudged Stephanie's neck with his nose. *Why don't you?*

Stephanie yelped. "I swear that dog knows everything we say."

Clara decided it was safer to ignore that remark. Instead, she started a conversation about the rodeo that lasted until they reached the resort.

The Hill Top Resort had prompted an outcry of protests when it was originally proposed, and even more as it was being built. In spite of several heated public meetings, presided over by Madeline Cheswick, the mayor of Finn's Harbor, and numerous demonstrations by enraged environmental groups, the resort had been completed on schedule.

Recently opened, it had failed to produce the kind of dire consequences envisioned by its critics. Although there were still those who grumbled about extra traffic in town and eyesores along the coast road, most residents of Finn's Harbor had settled down to an uneasy truce.

No one could deny the benefits brought about by the increase in tourists to the town, and the resort and accompanying golf course were too far along the coast to cause much of a physical nuisance.

The buildings were mostly hidden by trees from the road, and the golf course stretched inland, out of sight unless one was actually up on the bluff that housed the main structure.

Driving up the winding driveway that had been carved into the cliffs, Clara had to admit, the Hill Top was quite a magnificent sight. The green, multi-angled walls of the hotel blended in with the trees. Green and white striped canopies shaded every window. In front of the main doors, the sweeping drive curved around a bubbling water fountain.

Spread out on either side were smaller buildings, dotted with tiny balconies overlooking the sea with gorgeous views of the bay. The first tee of the golf course was visible from the driveway, the rest of the holes hidden by a thick stand of evergreens.

Clara felt as if she were looking at a movie set, and half expected to see famous stars wandering around.

Beside her, Stephanie was making oohing and aahing

noises, apparently every bit as impressed as her cousin. "I bet it costs an arm and a leg to stay here," she said, as Clara drove into the parking lot and parked the car.

"Probably." Clara wound down the windows, then twisted around to look at Tatters. "We won't be long. Be good and take care of the car."

Tatters grunted a response.

Clara patted his head before sliding out of the car. "We have to think of an excuse to talk to Paul Eastcott," she said, as Stephanie joined her.

"You waited until *now* to think of that?"

Clara started off toward the hotel. "Got any ideas?"

"We could say we're location scouts working for a movie company."

Clara glanced at her. "That's a pretty good idea."

"Except we don't have business cards, or anything."

"He might not ask for them."

"But what if he does?"

"Okay, what else?"

"I don't know. Something to do with the rodeo?"

Clara thought hard. "I guess we could ask him about becoming a barrel racer."

"Seriously? Do we look like women who ride horses every day?"

"We're not that out of shape."

"We're not exactly *in* shape, either. Besides, don't we have to apply to a rodeo association or something for that?"

"Okay, so what other brilliant ideas do you have?"

They had reached the doors, and now Stephanie looked worried. "We'd better think of something fast, or they'll be throwing us out on our ears."

"Okay, then. We fall back on the old reporter story." Clara's breath caught as she entered the lobby. Sparkling chandeliers hung from the ceiling, their light bouncing off the gold-papered walls. Green, polished leaves of English ivy wound around thick white pillars, and red velvet armchairs waited for tired bodies to sink into them.

Walking across the gold carpet felt like stepping on soft pillows, and she paused by a huge, ornate pot of orchids, fascinated by the brilliant hues of the delicate petals.

"This is a far cry from the sleazy taverns we usually end up in," Stephanie muttered, her gaze riveted on the far end of the lobby. "Get a load of that counter."

Clara looked. The reception desk stretched from wall to wall, its light oak surface gleaming in the glow from a dozen brass lamps. Behind it, young men and women in gold jackets smiled and nodded at customers, while behind them dozens of brightly colored fish swam back and forth in an enormous aquarium.

"It must have cost millions to build this place," Stephanie added. "I can see what Anita meant when she said Paul Eastcott wouldn't leave his wife. Her family must be disgustingly rich."

"Money isn't everything." Clara set off for the reception desk with her cousin at her heels.

The young man behind the counter bared his teeth in

a grin. "Good morning, ladies! Welcome to the fabulous Hill Top Resort. How can I be of service to you today?"

Clara gave him her sweetest smile. "We'd like a word with Mr. Paul Eastcott. Can you tell us where we can find him?"

The grin wavered. "Do you have an appointment?"

"No, but I'm sure he'd love to talk to us. We're planning on writing a glowing online review of the rodeo, and we'd like to interview him for the piece."

The grin faded away completely. "You'll have to make an appointment with him, Ms. . . .?"

"Quinn." Clara held out her hand. "Clara Quinn."

The young man looked up and down the counter as if uncertain what to do next. After brushing her fingers with his, he cleared his throat. "I'm sorry, Ms. Quinn, but—"

Stephanie leaned in next to her cousin, smiled up at the clerk and murmured in her best breathless, husky voice, "We simply *must* see him this morning. I'm sure he would want the rodeo to be successful, since he's responsible for producing it, and after the bad publicity it got yesterday with the murder and everything, we just *know* we have to put something positive out there as soon as possible so that people will flock back to the rodeo for the rest of its run and make it a *huge* success."

The clerk had the kind of panicked look one gets when faced with an impossible decision. "I still don't think—"

Stephanie held up her hand to silence him. "You look like the kind of man who knows how to make the right decision. Right now, Mr. Eastcott needs all the help he can get, and we're the right people to give it to him. I'm quite confident he'll thank you personally when he finds out how much we can do to boost the attendance at the rodeo."

"Really?" Again the young man looked right and left, as if seeking confirmation. All of his coworkers were deep in conversation with customers, however, while several more waited to be served. "I guess I could call him—"

His hand hovered over the phone and Stephanie covered it with hers. "That won't be necessary. I can see how busy you are, and I'm quite sure Mr. Eastcott will be delighted to talk to us. Just tell us where we can find his office."

She was practically purring, and the clerk visibly squirmed. His face still wreathed in doubt, he hesitated a few more seconds, then blurted out, "His office is on the eighth floor. Suite 880."

"Thank you so much." Stephanie flashed another smile, then tugged Clara's arm. "Let's go."

As they waited for the elevator, Clara said, "Haven't lost your touch, I see. You could charm the tusks off an elephant."

Stephanie grinned. "Just don't tell George that. I don't think he'd appreciate me making eyes at strange men to get what we want."

"Well, let's hope it works on Paul Eastcott."

Stephanie's grin vanished. "You think he's going to believe we'll write a review of the rodeo?"

"If we sound professional enough."

"What if he gets mad when he finds out we didn't do it?"

"There's no reason why we can't do it. There are plenty of social sites where we can write a review of the rodeo. After all, I've seen the show, and Wes told me a lot about it."

Stephanie flipped a strand of blonde hair back from her face. "Well, why didn't you say so? I've always fancied myself as a writer."

"Well now's your chance."

Neither of them spoke as they rode up to the eighth floor with a couple of chattering women and a stern-looking man in a business suit.

Stepping out of the elevator, Clara gazed in awe at the blue flocked wallpaper tinted with silver, the royal blue carpeting and the gold numbers and handles on each door they passed. "Everything smells so new," she murmured, as they walked the length of the corridor.

"Everything smells so *rich*." Stephanie paused at a water fountain where a miniature cherub offered a drink from a gold-tinted chalice. "Just look at that. Does water or wine come out of that thing?"

Clara chuckled. "You can check it out on the way back." She nodded at the last door on the right. "There it is. Suite 880."

Stephanie cleared her throat. "I hope he doesn't have us thrown out."

Clara lifted a hand to rap on the door. "That's the least of our worries."

Stephanie made a small sound in her throat as the door shot open and a man's face appeared in the gap.

Clara took a deep breath. The tall, husky man in front of her stared at her as if she were something nasty brought in on his shoe. He looked impatient, annoyed and inflexible. Here was a man obviously used to getting what he wanted and dealing harshly with anyone who tried to get in his way. Was he a killer? If so, she and Stephanie could be walking into a boatload of trouble.

6

Upon seeing the cousins, the man's dark eyebrows lowered. "Who are you? What do you want?"

Not too gracious a welcome, Clara thought, as she did her best to give him a professional smile. "Mr. Paul Eastcott?"

"I am." His frown intensified. "If you're looking for a job, you've come to the wrong place. My assistant, Lisa—" He shut his mouth, swallowed, cleared his throat and finally muttered, "Go back to the desk and ask—"

"Mr. Eastcott," Clara butted in, "we're so terribly sorry for your loss. We're huge fans of the rodeo and we just hate to see all the negative publicity about the murder, so we thought if we wrote a glowing review and put it out on the Web for everyone to see they would flock back to the rodeo to see what all the excitement is about."

Steely blue eyes regarded her with suspicion. "You're the press?"

"Freelance." Clara held out her hand. "I'm Clara Quinn and this is my . . . er . . . partner, Stephanie Dowd. We would love to write about the rodeo. It's such a thrilling show, and it would be a shame if people missed out on it because of such an unfortunate tragedy. I'm sure it cost a great deal to produce it, and you must worry about making a profit. With the right exposure, I'm confident the customers will be lining up to get in."

Paul Eastcott appeared to be thinking it over, and Clara pressed her advantage. "If you could just spare us a few minutes to answer a couple questions, we'd be so grateful. We do like to get our facts straight when we're writing reviews. Since you're the production manager, I'm sure you know more about the rodeo than anyone."

Paul opened the door a little wider. He wore a pale blue silk shirt under a well-tailored tan suit, and towered above Clara's five-feet-ten frame by at least six inches. His athletic build testified to a rigorous workout routine, and his strong features were clean-shaven. He looked the epitome of a successful and wealthy businessman, and just a little lethal. "What do you want to know?"

Taking that as an invitation, Clara brushed past him and marched into the office, dragging Stephanie by the arm. "Thank you so much. I promise we won't take up too much of your time."

Looking irritated, Paul closed the door. "Very well, but no questions about the murder. I know nothing about it, except what I heard from the media. I wasn't even there when it happened." He motioned to them to sit down on comfortable-looking leather swivel chairs in front of a wide, polished desk.

Taking a seat, Clara's gaze went to the windows, which reached from floor to ceiling and overlooked the golf course. The office was high enough to see over the trees, and in the distance, golf carts zipped between holes, or stood at greens while their occupants putted white balls across the smooth surface. A glittering blue lake divided some of the holes, and patches of golden sand gleamed in the sun. It looked peaceful, relaxing and expensive.

Stephanie sat down next to her, stiff-backed and look-ing poised for flight.

Grabbing the opening Paul Eastcott had given her, Clara murmured, "It must have been a dreadful shock for you to learn your assistant had been murdered."

"It was." Paul sat down behind the desk. "As I said, though, I wasn't here when it happened. I was in Port-land, trying to set up a run for the rodeo there."

"Oh, really? I hope you were successful." Belatedly, Clara realized she should have brought a notebook with her to take notes. Thinking fast, she drew her phone from her pocket and held it up. "Recorder. Hope that's okay?"

Paul answered her with a brief nod.

"So when did you hear about the murder, then?"

At first she thought he wasn't going to answer. His face seemed to lose all color, and he stared blankly down at his desk. Finally he spoke, his voice sounding strained. "I was on my way home that afternoon when I got a flat tire and had to stop to get it replaced. I knew I wouldn't have time to eat before the show, so I stopped at the Pioneer Inn for dinner. It took longer than I expected. By the time I got back on the road the show was almost over. I made it back just as the finale began. It was only a few minutes after the show ended when someone came to tell me Lisa's body had been found."

"That's terrible. You must have been devastated."

She was watching his face closely, but saw nothing but weariness in his expression when he answered. "I lost a good assistant, but her family lost so much more."

Either he was a good actor, or he wasn't as devoted to Lisa as she'd believed. Clara tried to sound unconcerned when she murmured, "I wonder who could have hated her enough to kill her."

Paul shifted his weight on the chair. "We don't know if it was someone who hated her. It could have been a robbery gone bad, a random act of violence—anything."

"So it could. Still, it seems that she must have been

planning on meeting someone. Why else would she go behind the concert stage?"

"Could have been any reason. I—" He broke off, as if realizing he'd said too much. "Okay, that's enough about the murder. I said no questions, remember? Now, what do you want to know about the rodeo?"

Realizing she would get no more out of him without raising his suspicions, Clara gave up on the line of questioning. Fortunately, thanks to Wes's descriptions, she was able to ask fairly intelligent questions about the performances and backstage production. When she figured she had enough to write a comprehensible overview of the entire process, she slipped her phone back in her pocket and stood up. "Thank you, Mr. Eastcott. I'm sure our readers will find this all very interesting."

"I hope so. We need this show to be successful if we want to make it an annual event."

"Then we'll certainly do our best to make the review as exciting as possible."

Stephanie, who had been silent throughout most of the conversation, murmured a polite good-bye. Clara led her out the door, thankful to be leaving.

Stephanie barely waited for the door to close behind them to whisper, "So? What do you think?"

Clara placed a finger over her lips and waited until they had almost reached the elevator before answering her. "I think Paul Eastcott probably cared for Lisa Warren, but that doesn't mean they were having an affair. Lisa could have just made that up. She wouldn't be the first woman to brag about a fictitious affair with a rich and powerful man. I did think it weird, though, that in spite of him asking us not to talk about the murder, he went ahead and told us what he was doing that evening. Unless he actually wanted us to put that in the review."

"Well, it does prove he had nothing to do with the murder. Maybe he just wants to clear his name with everyone."

"If it's true."

They had reached the elevator, and Stephanie jabbed the down button. "You think he was lying?"

"There's one way to find out." The doors silently slid open and Clara followed her cousin inside. This time they were alone, and Clara thumbed the button for the first floor.

"How?" Stephanie demanded, her gaze on the lit numbers display above the door.

"Eastcott said he stopped for dinner at the Pioneer Inn on the night Lisa was killed. I think it might be a good idea if we had dinner there. A man who looks like he does would stand out above the crowd. Someone was bound to have noticed him if he was there. I'll take that picture of him that was in the *Chronicle*."

Stephanie smiled as the doors eased open again. "The Pioneer Inn? I like it. *So* much better than the greasy food in cheap bars."

"If Paul was telling the truth about being at the inn that night, that would mean Lisa must have been meeting someone else behind the concert stage."

"Yeah. I wonder who."

"By the way, you didn't say a word while we were in his office. I kept expecting you to butt in with something."

Stephanie shivered. "He kind of intimidated me."

"That doesn't happen very often."

"I know. He seems so . . . powerful, I guess. Like there's nothing he couldn't or wouldn't do if he set his mind to it. That kind of man makes me nervous." Out in the fresh air, arms outstretched, she spun around. "This is such a beautiful place. It must be nice to live like this all the time."

Clara shook her head. "Too boring. You'd have nothing to get excited over."

Eyeing a couple of young, virile golfers strolling by, Stephanie murmured, "Oh, I don't know."

Clara gave her a hefty nudge in the shoulder. "You're a happily married woman with three kids."

"I am indeed." Stephanie grinned. "But it doesn't hurt to indulge in a little fantasy now and then, does it?"

"As long as it stays in your head." Clara set off for the car. "We'd better get a move on or Molly will be complaining because I'm late again."

"So when do we go to the Pioneer Inn?"

"How about tomorrow night? Since we close at six on Saturdays, we'll be able to make it there before seven if you meet me at the bookstore. We'll ask Molly to come along."

"Great! I'll tell George it's a girls' night out."

"Good thing you have a husband who doesn't mind being left alone with the kids."

Stephanie sighed. "I know. He's the best on earth. Then again, he has his golf days with his buddies, so he can't complain. Not that he ever does. Like I said. He's the best. Still, it wouldn't hurt to sweeten the deal."

She turned around and headed back toward the hotel.

"Where are you going?" After an anxious glance at her watch, Clara caught up with her. "You do know I'm supposed to be at the store in twenty minutes?"

"I do, and since I'm the boss, your job is pretty safe."

"Good to know. Why are we going back to the hotel?"

"I want to buy George a round of golf here. It will make up for me taking off tomorrow night." Once more they passed through the glass doors and walked across the plush carpet to the reception desk.

The same young man hurried over to them, an anxious frown on his face. "Is everything okay? Did you see Mr. Eastcott?"

"We did." Stephanie smiled. "He was very charming."

The clerk's shoulders relaxed. "Oh, thank God."

"I'd like to buy a round of golf for my husband." Stephanie fluttered her eyelashes. "Do you have any specials?"

The clerk raised his eyebrows. "You'd have to ask the pro shop about that."

He sounded as if the request was totally beneath him. It failed to intimidate Stephanie, though. She leaned across the counter and murmured, "Oh, I'm sure you could take care of it if you really wanted to, couldn't you?"

The young man straightened, cleared his throat then reluctantly picked up the phone.

Smiling, Clara leaned her back against the counter, prepared to enjoy one more look at the luxurious surroundings. A young couple caught her eye. They were sitting close together on two of the velvet armchairs. The guy was looking at his companion as if he had never seen anything more beautiful in his life.

Feeling a pang of envy, Clara turned her gaze to the doors just in time to see Paul Eastcott pause in front of them. Instead of going outside, however, he beckoned to a young woman in a gold jacket who was crossing the foyer.

She looked nervous as she approached Paul, and apparently for good cause. It was obvious the manager was upset about something. He waved his arm at her and raised his voice so every word was audible across the busy room. "I've told you before about talking on the job. I won't tolerate such behavior. Get out now and don't come back."

The woman began explaining something too quietly

to be heard, but Paul cut her off. "I don't want to hear any excuses. You're fired. Now get out. And don't expect any references."

By now just about everyone's head was turned toward the unfortunate woman. She took one look around her and promptly burst into tears.

Furious that the man had humiliated his employee in front of everyone, Clara had to fight the urge to run over and comfort the poor woman. Stephanie had turned around at the sound of the argument and was scowling at Paul as if she'd like to hit him. "What a jerk," she muttered. "Someone should teach him how to treat his staff."

"I have your tee time," the clerk said behind them. He thrust the slip of paper at Stephanie, who swung back to face him with a smile.

"Thank you so much. You've been so nice. I'll be sure to tell Mr. Eastcott how helpful you've been."

The young man sent a hasty glance at the doors, through which Paul had now vanished. "Please don't," he said, sounding worried. "Just leave. Please?"

Stephanie raised her eyebrows, shrugged then slipped the paper into her purse. Turning, she murmured to Clara, "Some people can be so disagreeable."

Following her cousin through the doors, Clara wondered if she'd meant the clerk or Paul Eastcott. One thing she did know: In her opinion, Paul Eastcott seemed a far more likely killer than the affable Wes Carlton. He had a temper—and a complete disregard for people's feelings.

Or did she just want it to be Paul, rather than Wes? It would certainly let her off the hook as far as exposing a killer to Dan.

Letting out a sigh, she reminded herself how dumb it would be to let her worries over Rick's feelings cloud her judgment. A woman's life had been cut short, and whoever did it deserved to pay the price. Even if it turned out to be Rick's best buddy.

"I'm glad I don't work for Paul Eastcott," Stephanie said, as they hurried over to the parking lot. "He sounds like a lousy boss."

"Well, that's the nice thing about owning your own business." Reaching the car, Clara paused to get her breath. "You don't have to answer to anyone."

"Except the tax man." Stephanie opened her door. "And George. I can handle him, though. The tax man, I'm not so sure."

Grinning, Clara opened the door and slid onto her seat.

Tatters grunted as she closed the door. *About time.*

Clara reached out a hand behind her to pat his head. "Sorry, boy."

"I wish I could have seen the rodeo," Stephanie said, as Clara drove out of the parking lot and onto the coast road. "After listening to Paul Eastcott talk about it, it all sounds so exciting. I never realized just how much goes into one of those shows."

"You could get your chance if we don't find out something useful soon. We might have to go back there to talk to some more of the people who knew Lisa."

"Count me in! Now, what are you going to do about the review you're supposed to write?"

"I thought *we* were going to write it together."

Stephanie pulled a face. "You're so much better at that stuff than I am."

"Flattery is not going to get you out of it." Clara turned off the coast road and headed into town. "What happened to 'I've always fancied myself as a writer'?"

"That was before I got a load of Big Shot Paul Eastcott." Stephanie shuddered. "I can just imagine how he'd react if he didn't like the review."

"Well, he doesn't scare me. We're just repeating what he told us, anyway."

Stephanie was silent for a moment. "Are you going to put in all that stuff about his not being there when Lisa was killed?"

"I'm not even going to mention the murder." Clara sighed, realizing she'd just committed herself to writing the piece alone.

"Yeah, good thinking. If Dan saw it he'd know we were butting our noses in again, as he so graciously puts it."

"He's probably going to know anyway. If he and Tim are still investigating, we're bound to run into one another sooner or later."

"Well, so far he hasn't thrown us in jail."

"There's always a first time."

Stephanie glanced at her watch. "Crap. Is that the time? I'd better leave straight from the parking lot. I'll call you later to see how things are going."

Clara nodded, her mind already creating the opening lines of her review. If they didn't get too busy that afternoon she could work on it, and might even get it up online when she got home.

The moment she parked the car, Stephanie scrambled out. "See you later," she called out, and tore across the parking lot to where she'd parked her SUV. The last Clara saw of her cousin, she was roaring out onto the road and down the hill.

Molly was behind the counter serving a customer when Clara walked into the bookstore. She nudged her head at the aisles and mouthed two words. *Reading Nook.*

Immediately on guard, Clara headed down the aisle. She wasn't too surprised to see Dan Petersen seated on an armchair in the Nook, a mug of coffee in one hand and a half-eaten donut in the other.

He looked up as she approached, and gave her a hard stare from under his bushy brows. Dan had been Finn's Harbor's police chief for a good many years before Clara returned home from New York. Despite his gruff manner, the townsfolk seemed to like him. People spoke well of him, praising him for his obvious dedication to the safety and well-being of the general public.

He was there to serve, he'd said once, in a brief speech

at one of the town meetings, and it was obvious to everyone that's what he tried to do. They knew the concerns of the residents of Finn's Harbor would always be his top priority. He'd proven that on several occasions, earning in turn the public's respect.

His relationship with the cousins had been rocky ever since they had solved a murder that had taken place in the Raven's Nest. Clara suspected his irritation at their "interference" in his investigation was due more to concern for their safety than any hindrance they might have been. After all, the cousins had helped to solve more than one murder, thanks mostly to Clara's detested gift of the Quinn Sense.

Although he'd never said as much, Clara knew Dan was baffled by the cousins' success in tracking down a criminal, when his own efforts and that of his department had been less than fruitful. Since she wasn't able to enlighten him, she hoped he'd put it down to dumb luck.

Right now, he wasn't looking too happy. "Tim tells me you've been pestering the rodeo folk about the murder."

Clara walked over to the sink and reached in the overhead cabinet for a mug. Filling it with coffee, she murmured, "Has someone been complaining?"

"Not as far as I know. That's not the point."

She carried the mug over to a chair opposite him and

sat down. "I'm writing an online review of the rodeo, and needed some facts about it." It was the truth, after all, she thought, and he could hardly give her a hard time for that.

Dan's blue eyes were slits in his round face. "Facts about the rodeo, or the murder?"

"I'm not writing a review of the murder."

She met his keen gaze without flinching, and finally he leaned back in his chair with a sigh. "Lady, you and your cousin will be the death of me."

She smiled. "I certainly hope not."

He took a swallow of his coffee and balanced the mug on his belly. "I'm only going to say this once. Stay out of trouble and leave the police work to me and my crew. Okay? You've been lucky in the past. Sooner or later that luck is going to run out. I don't want to be the one who has to tell your folks you're not coming home."

Clara felt a sting of apprehension. "I promise you, Dan, I'll do my best to stay out of trouble."

"Good." He finished his donut in one bite and stood up. "That goes for your scatterbrained cousin as well."

Stephanie would not appreciate that, Clara thought, with a flash of amusement. "I'll be sure to pass that along."

He handed her his mug, turned to leave then looked back at her. "I don't suppose you picked up anything useful while you were asking questions out there?"

She tried to look innocent. "Lots of useful stuff. Like how fast the horses go when they're charging around the barrels in a figure eight, how calf ropers tie their pigging strings and—"

"Okay, okay." Dan held up his hand. "Just try and remember that murder is a serious business. You've had some close calls in the past. Don't make me have to put you two in custody to keep you safe."

He was gone before she could answer. Clara let out the breath she hadn't realized she was holding. Tim must have seen her and Stephanie that morning at the rodeo, or maybe at the resort. She'd have to be more careful about how and where she talked to people.

A rush of tourists kept her and Molly busy throughout the afternoon, giving her no opportunity to work on her review. It was almost time for Molly to leave before the last customer wandered out of the bookstore with a pile of books under her arm.

"I unpacked the boxes Stephanie wanted opened," Molly said, arriving at the counter in her usual breathless manner. "There's a bit more room in the stockroom now."

Clara took the pile of books from her and put them on the counter. "I'll get these out on the shelves later." She hesitated, then added, "Did you hear any noises while you were in there?"

Molly gazed blankly at her. "Noises?"

Feeling a bit paranoid, Clara flapped a hand at her. "Oh, it's okay. Forget it. I thought I heard something moving about in there, but it's probably my imagination."

Now Molly looked worried. "I didn't hear anything."

"It's okay. It was probably the wind or something." Clara straightened the pile of books. "So what do you think of this new series?"

"I can't believe how popular it is." Molly held up one of the books. A green and gold dragon with flames gushing from his mouth decorated the cover, while a young man dressed in a red and black tunic brandished a sword over its head. "It looks totally gory to me. All that blood and guts everywhere. Ugh!"

"People don't read those books for the battles. They read them for the romance." Clara pointed to the cover. "Look at the blonde hovering behind his shoulder."

"Oh." Molly looked. "Well, that makes it better, I guess, though I can't see anything romantic about plunging a sword in an animal's gut. Give me a ghost story any time. Ghosts can't get physical."

Clara grinned. "You must not be reading the latest ghost romances."

"What?" Molly looked horrified. "Don't tell me."

"Okay, I won't." Clara looked up at the new clock on the wall. She'd bought it for Stephanie's birthday, which coincided with the anniversary of the store's opening. The clock had a witch's face, complete with black hat. As the second hand ticked around, the witch's eyes blinked in time, and when the hand reached twelve, the eyes glowed red for five seconds.

There had been many times when Clara had waited in vain for payment while the fascinated customer watched the second hand tick out the minute until the witch's eyes turned red. That was when Clara wished she'd never bought the thing.

"I need to run over to Rick's store," she said. "Can you hold the fort for ten minutes?"

"Sure." Molly pointed to the untidy shelves. "I'll straighten up this mess before you get back."

Clara smiled. "You're an angel. By the way, I haven't had time to ask you yet. Steffie and I are having dinner at the Pioneer Inn tomorrow night. Would you like to come along?"

Molly gasped. "Seriously? I'd *love* to go! Brad's in Portland job hunting and won't be back until Sunday. I was just getting mopey thinking about spending the weekend alone. This is *great*! You can tell me how the murder investigation is going."

"Shhh!" Clara looked around, thankful to be reassured that no one was in the store. "Don't mention to anyone that we're looking into it. Dan will go ballistic if he finds out."

"Oh, right. Sorry." Molly drew her fingers across her closed lips. "Not a word. I swear."

"Okay. I won't be long." Wasting no more time, Clara flew across the road to the hardware store.

Tyler gave her a lopsided grin when she walked through the door. He always seemed anxious when he saw her, probably because she invariably did or said something weird when she was around Rick.

She greeted him with a smile, hoping to put him at ease. "Is Rick around?"

Tyler jerked a thumb over his shoulder. "In the office. He's got company, though."

"Oh." She hesitated, wondering if she should come back later.

"It's that rodeo guy who's supposed to have murdered that woman."

That settled it. Without wasting another moment, Clara headed for the office.

Tapping on the door, she jumped when it opened immediately. She saw Wes first, then Rick standing behind him. "Sorry," she said, "am I disturbing something?"

"Nope. Wes was just leaving." Rick opened the door wider. "Come on in."

Nodding at Wes, Clara stepped into the office. "I'm glad I caught you. I wanted to ask you a question."

Wes glanced at Rick, his face a mask of doubt.

"It's okay," Rick said. "She's trying to help you." He placed his arm around Clara's shoulders and gave her a hug. "Wes got cut from the competition. He was told he couldn't compete while he was being investigated by the police. So he needs all the help he can get. Did you find out anything?"

"Not much." Wes still looked uneasy, so she turned her attention to him. "I was out at the rodeo this morning, asking a few questions. I talked to Anita, Melosa and Paul Eastcott."

Wes looked worried. "You talked to Eastcott? What did he say?"

"Not a lot." She concentrated on Wes's face. "Was Lisa having an affair with Paul Eastcott?"

She heard Rick's swift intake of breath, but she was busy watching Wes. Shock, anger and sorrow followed in quick succession as the emotions swept across his face. Finally he lifted his shoulders in what was obviously a calculated shrug. "I have no idea. Lisa didn't confide in me."

"But you must have heard people talking."

His eyes were hard when he looked at her. "I don't listen to gossip."

She tried another tack. "Paul said he wasn't at the rodeo when the murder happened, so I'm assuming no one saw him that night."

"I don't remember seeing him." Wes shook his head. "I don't remember too much about that night. All I can think about is Anita telling me that Lisa had been murdered."

"When did she tell you that?"

Wes frowned. "I guess it was right after they found Lisa's body. I remember hearing the sirens as I was running over to the stage."

"Can you remember anyone else who was there at the scene?"

"The cops were sending people away when I got there. Some of the rodeo folk were there, but I don't remember which ones."

"Must have been a helluva shock," Rick said.

"Yeah." Wes hunched his shoulders. "It was even more of a shock when the cops took me in for questioning."

"I know exactly how that feels." Rick tightened his hold on Clara. "It happened to me not so long ago, and thanks to this beautiful lady here, it all turned out okay."

Wes's gaze raked Clara's face. "You're a detective?"

She laughed. "No, just nosy. I ask a lot of questions and sometimes get the right answers."

"Well, I'd sure appreciate it if you could get the right answers for me."

"I'll certainly do my best."

"Thanks." He hesitated, then added, "I'm not the only one who can't account for my time during the murder. It happened in between events, and as far as I know, the only one in the arena when Lisa was killed was Sparky. I was signing autographs and talking to fans. Everyone else was somewhere else. If it weren't for that pigging string and the argument I had with Lisa that afternoon, the cops would have had no reason to question me. Now I've lost my shot in the competition, and this could wreck my career."

"Hang in there, buddy," Rick said, looking worried. "Sooner or later the cops will find out who did it."

"Let's hope it's sooner." Wes held out his hand to Rick. "Thanks, buddy. It helps to know someone believes me."

Rick shook his hand. "Come in any time. How about we grab a beer or two tomorrow night? I close up early on Saturdays."

Wes managed a tired smile. "Sounds good to me."

Rick tapped his fingers on Clara's shoulder. "Wanna come?"

"Can't. I'm having dinner with Steffie tomorrow." Clara looked at Wes. "One last question. Melosa told me that Anita stole a red shirt from you."

He snorted in disgust. "That woman is nuts. It's my lucky shirt. The second it went missing I knew who had taken it. She's taken stuff of mine before. I got it back, though."

"When did she take it?"

"The first day we got here. I'd washed it and hung it outside the trailer and she grabbed it. I went after her as soon as I realized it was missing."

Rick chuckled. "He was wearing it that night, remember?"

"Yes," Clara said slowly. "I do."

Wes gave her an odd look. "I'd better get going." He waved a hand at Rick. "See you tomorrow night, then?"

"Yeah. I'll pick you up at the trailer."

With another nod at both of them, Wes disappeared.

Letting Clara go, Rick walked over to the wall behind his desk. "What was all that about a red shirt?"

She watched him unpin a sheet of paper from the wall and slip it into his desk drawer. "Oh, nothing, really. Melosa told me about the shirt and I wondered if it was significant in some way, that's all. By the way, what kind of car does Wes drive?"

"He drives a truck, like most of the rodeo guys." He stared at her for a long moment. "You think Wes killed Lisa."

It was more of a statement than a question, and she was quick to answer. "I learned a long time ago not to take anything for granted. You asked me to look into the murder, and that's what I'm doing."

"Hey. Wait a minute." He skirted his desk and hurried over to her. "I asked you to talk to Anita. I definitely remember saying I didn't want you tracking down a killer. Why were you talking to Paul Eastcott, anyway?"

"Anita told me that Lisa said he was having an affair with her. Though Anita seemed to think it was wishful thinking on Lisa's part. I wanted to know if they really were involved."

"So did you find out?"

"Nope. Not yet, anyway. He seemed nervous when I mentioned Lisa, but he said he was at the Pioneer Inn when Lisa was killed, so I didn't pursue it."

Rick frowned. "You wouldn't be going to the Pioneer Inn with Stephanie tomorrow night, by any chance?"

Clara shrugged. "It's supposed to be a great place to eat."

Rick took hold of her shoulders. "Clara, promise me you won't go asking any more questions. I'm worried about Wes, sure, but I'm far more worried that you'll end up in some kind of trouble. You did what I asked and talked to Anita. Now leave it alone and let the cops deal with it. Please?"

She patted the hand on her shoulder. "I'm just going to dinner, Rick. That's all."

He looked deep into her eyes. "Why doesn't that make me feel better?"

She laughed. "Guess you'll just have to trust me."

Placing an arm around her shoulders, he gave her a hug. "I do. You're sure you can't come with us tomorrow night?"

"Nope." She smiled. "I'll take a rain check, though."

"You've got it. Cash it soon, okay? Dinner at my place?"

For a brief instant she was tempted to invite him home for dinner. Then the image of her mother's eager face flashed into her mind, and the impulse vanished. "It's a date. Now I have to get back to the store. Molly's waiting to go home."

Rick heaved an exaggerated sigh. "Always running after someone, somewhere."

"Yep, that's me." She left, waving at Tyler as she flew by him.

Pausing on the sidewalk for the traffic to clear, she recalled the vision she'd had of someone in a red shirt standing over Lisa's body. If she discovered it was Wes, how could she report it to Dan, knowing how much it would devastate Rick?

Sending up a silent prayer that her suspicions were unfounded, she crossed the road and headed back to the store.

7

The evening lull in customers gave Clara an opportunity to work on her review, and by closing time she had a pretty good rough draft. Deciding to run it by Stephanie before doing any more to it, she sent the file to her e-mail and closed up shop.

Jessie was waiting for her when she arrived home. She'd barely set foot in the door when her mother called out to her.

Tatters bounded toward her as she walked into the living room, where her mother sat in front of the TV, her usual wineglass at her elbow.

Clara bent down and patted the dog's head.

Tatters shot up his jaw and deposited a wet lick on her nose. *About time you got home. I'm going stir-crazy in here.*

"I'll take you for a walk after dinner."

"Are you talking to me or the dog?" Jessie asked, sounding snippy.

Clara sighed. "Sorry. Did you want something?"

"Just to tell you that Seth Ferguson was killed last night."

Clara felt as if all the blood had drained out of her head. Seth was the owner of the boating supplies store just down the street from the bookstore. She waved to him just about every morning while walking past his store to the Raven's Nest. He'd often come into the bookstore for a cup of coffee and a Danish, and never left without buying a book.

"Seth? What happened?"

Her mother looked as shocked as she felt. "He was run over in the parking lot of Harry's Pub, out on the coast road." Jessie's eyes filled with tears. "I was just talking to Grace in the library the other day. She adored her husband. She must be devastated."

Clara went immediately to her mother and put both arms around her. It hadn't been that long since Clara's father had died, and she knew his loss was still fresh in Jessie's mind. Hearing of her friend's loss must have brought it all back. "I'm so sorry, Mother."

Jessie nodded, hunting for a tissue from a box on the table at her side. "Poor Grace. What will she do without him?"

Clara let her go and picked up the empty wineglass. "I'll get you some more wine."

She hurried into the kitchen and opened the fridge. Taking out the half-full bottle of wine, she tried to make sense of what she'd just heard. Her hand shook as she poured the golden liquid into the glass.

How could her visions have been so wrong? She had seen the accident in her head, but she'd seen a clown tumbling through the air. Not Seth. What had the Sense been trying to tell her?

Carrying the glass back to her mother, she said quietly, "You heard about it on the news?"

"No." Jessie took the glass from her. "Grace's daughter, Nancy, called me. I was supposed to have lunch with Grace tomorrow, so Nancy called to cancel. I knew as soon as I heard her voice that something was wrong. She cried when she told me what happened. I couldn't believe it. She said it was a hit-and-run. The driver just took off and never stopped, the miserable coward. The police are looking for him now. Someone saw a truck racing away from the scene, but didn't get the license plate."

A truck. Everything in her vision fit, except that it wasn't Marty who had died in that parking lot. It was a good friend. A loving husband and father.

Tatters whined, and Clara gathered her thoughts. "Have you had dinner yet?" She laid a hand on her mother's shoulder. "Can I get you anything?"

Jessie blew her nose. "I've already eaten. There's a casserole in the fridge. You just have to heat it up in the microwave."

Right then Clara had no appetite for dinner. She needed to get out in the fresh air and clear her head. Her mother, however, had gone to the trouble of cooking for her, and she wasn't about to disappoint her.

Seated in the kitchen, she tried to ignore Tatters' longing looks while she ate a fair portion of the casserole. Her mother was a great cook, and usually Clara enjoyed the meals, but tonight the food tasted like shredded paper, and even the glass of wine she'd poured for herself tasted sour.

Again and again she replayed her vision in her mind. There was no doubt she'd been looking at Marty lying in that parking lot. The black and white costume, the spiderweb lines drawn around the huge red eyes—there was no mistaking the clown.

Had the accident in her vision not yet happened? Would there be another one? In the next instant she was cursing her overactive brain. It was all this Quinn Sense stuff—it was playing havoc with her mind. Making her dream up all kinds of unrealistic scenarios. She was upset over Seth's death. That was all. As for her vision, it wasn't the first time the Sense had got things wrong, and it probably wouldn't be the last.

After slipping some of the casserole into Tatters' dish, she rinsed off her plate and glass and stuck them in the dishwasher.

Her mother was watching the news when she went out into the living room. "I haven't seen anything yet," she told Clara. "I guess it's old news already."

"Well, let me know if they do report it. I'm taking Tatters for a walk. I won't be long."

"Go ahead." Jessie took a deep sip of wine. "Take that mutt out of here. He's beginning to smell."

Hey! You would smell too, if you hadn't had a bath in weeks.

"I'll give him a bath on my next day off," Clara said, fixing a stern glare at the dog.

Tatters grunted, and padded to the door.

The night had closed in when Clara stepped outside, the streetlamps casting an orange glow on the sidewalk. Walking fast, with Tatters straining at the leash, she reached the harbor and paused at the steps leading to the beach.

Walking the sands at night was not one of her favorite things to do, but Tatters loved to run free without his leash, and the beach was one of the few places he could enjoy that freedom. Luckily the moon was bright enough that she could see right down to the water's edge, and the scattered bonfires farther down the shore reassured her. Unsnapping Tatters' leash from his collar, she murmured, "There you go, boy."

Tatters shot down the steps and scampered across the sand to the water. Following more slowly, Clara tried to erase the vision that persisted in haunting her. She still found it hard to accept that it was Seth Ferguson and not Marty Pearce lying in that parking lot with the life seeping out of him.

She didn't know Grace that well, but somehow she felt duty-bound to call on her and offer her condolences. Perhaps she and her mother could go together. Jessie would like that.

Feeling a little better, she watched Tatters splashing several yards away into the water, only to turn tail and race madly out onto the soft sand. He rolled onto his back, legs waving in the air as he wriggled from side to side. Clara closed her eyes, envisioning the struggle she'd have to get all the sand out of his shaggy hair before she could take him inside the house.

When she opened her eyes again, Tatters had vanished.

At first she couldn't believe it. Peering into the shadows, she whistled, hoping to see his dark silhouette against the flickering flames of the bonfires. Nothing moved on that dark stretch of sand.

Where could he possibly have gone so fast? She'd heard no sound, except for the waves slapping the shore. Cupping her hands to her mouth, she called out his name. Ears straining for his answering bark, she stared at the churning ocean. Had he gone back into the water? Was he right now being swept out to sea, never to be seen again?

Horror gripped her heart. Not Tatters. Not Rick's dog.

She started to run toward the water, shouting his name over and over. Stumbling in the sand, she fell to her knees, tears starting down her cheeks. It was in that moment that she realized how much she loved that dog. He wasn't Rick's dog anymore. He was hers. Not just a dog, but a friend. Family. She couldn't lose him. She just couldn't.

———

"Clara invited me out to dinner tomorrow night," Stephanie said, handing her husband a beer. "We're going to the Pioneer Inn."

George took the can and flipped open the tab. "That's a pretty fancy restaurant. What's the occasion?"

"Nothing special." Stephanie sat down on the couch next to him, avoiding his gaze. "You're not watching the news?"

"I was just going to turn it on." He reached for the remote, but kept it in his hand without turning on the TV. "You two don't usually go for the expensive night out."

Knowing she was not going to escape his questions that easily, Stephanie shrugged. "We haven't been out together in a while. Clara wanted to take me somewhere nice for a treat. Neither of us have eaten at the Pioneer Inn, so we thought we'd go there."

George narrowed his eyes. "This wouldn't have anything to do with the murder of that woman at the rodeo, would it?"

Stephanie opened her eyes wide. "The murder? Whatever made you think of that?"

"Just a lucky guess. Knowing how you two love to go

sleuthing, I figured a night out together probably had a connection somewhere."

Stephanie shook her head. "We're just going for a nice dinner." She met her husband's gaze and faltered. "Maybe ask a few questions, that's all."

"Uh-huh. I thought so." George hit a button on the remote with his thumb. "Just promise me you'll stay out of trouble, okay?"

"Of course. I—" She broke off as the voice of Spencer Barnes, the local news anchor, resonated in the quiet room. "Did he just say what I think he said?" She stared at the screen, unwilling to accept the words she'd heard.

"Oh God." George turned up the sound, though it was already drumming in her ears.

"Ferguson was pronounced dead at the scene," Spencer Barnes announced, sounding remarkably unmoved by the awful news. "The police are looking for the truck involved in the hit-and-run."

"No, it can't be. Not Seth." Stephanie burst into tears and buried her face in her husband's shoulder. Poor Seth. Poor Grace. It was just too much to bear thinking about.

———

Fighting the panic threatening to overwhelm her, Clara struggled to her feet. She couldn't leave the beach without knowing what had happened to Tatters. Even if she stayed all night. Maybe he would swim back with the tide. Maybe he was out there, struggling to fight the surge of water taking him out to sea.

She took a step toward the water, then paused as she heard a faint bark. It seemed to have come from somewhere behind the rocks. Could it be?

Hope spurring her on, she tore up the sand toward a crop of craggy rocks. The barking was louder now, and she was almost certain it was Tatters. Her lungs ached and her ragged breathing made her voice hoarse as once more she shouted his name.

This time his bark answered her, and she heard the words in her head. *Help! Over here!*

She scrambled around the rocks to where a patch of sand lay between the boulders. Tatters stood with his legs spread apart, tufts of hair in a ridge down his back. Lying in front of him was a man. Someone she recognized. "It's all right, Tats," she said quietly. "He's a friend."

"Thank the good Lord," Marty Pearce said, sounding a little strained. "I thought your dog was going to attack me."

Tatters, quiet now, sat down on his haunches. *Thanks for nothing.*

"What happened?" Clara hurried over to Marty. "Are you all right?"

"Yeah, I guess. I tripped over a rock. Twisted my bum leg." He held out his hand. "Give me a hand up?"

Clara grasped the calloused hand and tugged.

Grunting, Marty climbed to his feet. "I was trying to get up when this hound came bounding in here barking his head off. I was afraid to move in case he lunged at me."

"He would never do that," Clara assured the clown. "He was trying to attract my attention by barking, that's all. He was trying to help you."

"Oh." Marty sent a wary glance at the dog. "Well, thanks."

Yeah. Well, okay.

Clara looked down at Marty's leg. "Does it hurt much? Can you walk?"

"I guess so." He tested his foot and grimaced. "I might need some help, though."

"Here." She offered him her arm. "Where's your car?"

"Up on the road, just a little ways down. When the show ended, I figured I'd take a stroll on the beach before I settled in for the night. Should have known better than to try it in the dark." He winced as he hobbled alongside her. "I might as well have gone down to the tavern again."

Her arm jerked under his. "You were at a tavern last night?"

He paused for just a second or two, as if he were surprised by her question. "Yep. There was no show last night, so a bunch of us went down there."

She tried to calm her voice. "I bet that was fun. Which one did you go to?"

"Er . . . Wally's Pub, or Terry's Pub, something like that."

"Harry's Pub? Out on the coast road?"

"That's the one." He sounded out of breath as they climbed the steps. "You know it?"

"I know of it." She hesitated, then added, "There was a fatal accident there last night."

He stopped short, staring at her as if she'd announced the end of the world. "An accident?"

"A hit-and-run. A friend of mine was killed."

"You kidding me? Hell, that's a real bummer." He squeezed her arm. "Must have happened after we left. Or most of us, anyway." He shook his head. "Some of those cowboys can drink all night long and wake up feeling just fine. Me? Three's the limit or I'm a basket case all next day."

Clara paid little attention to what he was saying. The news that Marty and some of the rodeo guys were at the bar the night Seth was killed raised a chilling possibility. What if Seth's death wasn't an accident? What if someone had intended to kill Marty and had killed Seth by mistake? They were both roughly the same height and weight, and it was dark in the parking lot.

Clara froze. If she was right, whoever wanted to harm the clown would realize he'd killed the wrong man, and could still be after Marty. "Can you remember who was there when you left? Was anyone wearing a red shirt?"

The words had popped out before she'd had time to think. Marty let go of her arm and stepped away from her. After an awkward pause, he asked quietly, "Okay, so what's this all about?"

To cover her confusion, she ordered Tatters to come

over to her, then bent down and fastened his leash. When she straightened again, she found Marty staring at her, tension lining his face.

She searched her mind for several long seconds, trying to find the right words without giving too much away. "Two deaths in as many nights is unnerving," she said at last. "I just think you should be very careful and stay on guard. Don't go out alone again at night."

Marty's frown deepened. "You sound like my mother. What makes you think I'm in some kind of danger?"

"I think everyone connected to the rodeo is in danger until Lisa's killer is found."

He nodded, slowly, as if thinking things over. "Are you telling me your friend's death wasn't an accident?"

"I didn't say that."

He stared at her long enough to make her uncomfortable. "If it was one of our guys who ran down your friend, and I hope to high heaven it wasn't, he was most likely drunk and didn't see the guy in the dark. Let's hope he owns up to his mistake and takes his punishment like a man. As for whoever murdered Lisa, I'd say he's probably hightailed it out of town and is far away by now. The cops will catch up with him eventually. They always do."

"I hope you're right." Clara tugged on Tatters' leash as he strained to walk down the street.

"My truck's right down here." Marty nodded at a pickup parked at the curb. "Good thing it's not a stick shift. I only need one foot to drive it."

"Will you be okay?" Clara looked anxiously at the truck. "I don't have my car here, but if you want to wait while I go get it—"

"Thanks, but I'll be just fine." He patted her arm. "You've been a good pal, and I appreciate it." He looked down at Tatters and tentatively held out his hand. The dog ignored it, and after a moment, Marty pulled his hand back. "Lucky for me you were out here."

"We usually go for a walk around this time." Clara laid a hand on Tatters' neck. "I'm just happy we were able to help. I hope your leg's okay."

"Thanks to you and your dog, there's not much harm done. A night's rest and I'll be good to go tomorrow."

"You might want to get it looked at," Clara called out after him as he limped off.

He answered her with a wave of his hand, and she watched him until he hauled himself into his truck and drove away.

Jessie had gone to bed when Clara arrived home, and she had to spend twenty minutes in the utility room combing sand out of Tatters' coat before she could let him into her bedroom. The dog slept with her on her bed, much to her mother's disgust, and Clara had no wish to spend the night brushing sand off the covers.

Tatters wasn't too happy with all the attention, and kept shifting away from her. "Stand still," she told him, hauling him closer for the fourth time. "You're not going to sleep until I get all this stuff out of your coat."

Bummer.

She eased the comb through the tangled fur. "You need a bath."

No kidding.

"You did good tonight, Tats. Rescuing Marty like that. Though you could have been a bit more sociable. He's a nice man."

Tatters grunted.

Clara shook the comb on the sheet of newspaper she'd spread on the floor. "I know you prefer females, but it wouldn't hurt you to be a bit nicer to the men you meet."

Tatters grunted again.

Thinking about Marty brought back their conversation. Maybe he was right. Maybe Seth's death had been nothing more than an accident. Maybe the clown wasn't in danger after all. But there was that vision she'd had of him tumbling down the steps at the rodeo.

She paused, holding the comb above Tatters' fur. As if sensing her preoccupation, the dog moved slowly out of reach.

Barely noticing, Clara recalled the vision. Could it be that Marty's fall down the steps was nothing more than his tripping over the rocks tonight? Maybe her interpretations of the visions were exaggerated.

She had to stop worrying about the clown and concentrate on finding out more about Lisa's death. So far it seemed the police were having no luck in finding the killer. Maybe Marty was right, and he'd already left town.

Maybe it was someone with no connections to the rodeo. After all, Lisa lived in Mittleford now. It could have been anyone who hated her enough to kill her. If only she could find out who Lisa was meeting behind the concert stage that night . . .

Hey!

Clara jumped. Apparently Tatters was getting tired of being ignored. "Okay, okay. I guess I'm done. But heaven help you if I wake up tomorrow with a bed full of sand. I don't know why you have to roll in it, anyway. You—"

She broke off as Jessie's voice called out from the hallway. "Clara? Is that you?"

No, it's the tooth fairy.

Ignoring the dog, Clara pushed the door open wider. "I'm coming. I was just cleaning off Tatters."

Jessie appeared in front of her, dressed in a robe, her face covered in a white cream. "I heard you talking. I thought maybe you'd brought someone home with you."

The wistful note in her voice told Clara her mother had hoped the someone was Rick. "No, just Tatters."

"Talking to that dog again. One of these days you'll do that in public and someone will call 911."

Clara smiled. "I'm glad you're up. I wanted to ask you if you'd like to see Grace tomorrow. We could go together. Take her a card or something."

"Don't you have to work?"

"Not until noon, and you don't have to go to the library. I'll get up early."

Jessie's eyes misted. "Really? I'd like that. We should probably call her first, though."

"I'll let you do that." Clara glanced at her watch. "I have to call Steffie now before she goes to bed." She planted a quick kiss on her mother's cheek. "Sleep well."

"You, too." Jessie disappeared into her room and Clara led Tatters into her own bedroom, closing the door quietly behind him.

He immediately jumped on the bed and settled down, his head on his paws, his brown eyes watching her.

Sitting down at her small desk, Clara turned on her computer and brought up the file she'd sent from the bookstore. Then she dialed Stephanie's number and waited.

Her cousin answered almost at once. "Have you heard the news?" she demanded, before Clara had a chance to say anything.

"If you're talking about Seth Ferguson's accident, then yes."

"It's just terrible. Whoever did it never even stopped. His family must be in agony."

"I know. Jessie and I are going to see Grace tomorrow morning. Do you want to come with us?"

"Can't. Molly won't be in tomorrow. She's got the stomach flu—or maybe it's something she ate."

"Oh, sorry about that." Clara hesitated. "Do you want me to come in early?"

"No, I'll manage until you get there. It's good that you're going to see Seth's wife. Tell her how sorry I am."

"I will. Do you have a minute to listen to the review? I wrote a rough draft tonight."

"Oh, okay. Shoot."

Reading from the computer screen, Clara recited what she'd written.

"Sounds good," Stephanie declared when she was done. "I don't think Paul Eastcott will complain about that. Where are you going to post it?"

"On the city council's website. On that page where they ask for people's opinions on various events."

"Oh, yeah. Do you think he'll see it on there, though?"

"It doesn't really matter. I told him I'd write the review. I never said where I was going to post it."

"Oh, right."

"By the way, I ran into Marty Pearce tonight on the beach."

"The clown? Was he in costume? Ugh! How creepy."

"No, he wasn't." Clara repeated as much of the conversation as she could remember.

"Wow." Stephanie sounded uneasy. "You don't really think someone deliberately ran down Seth, thinking he was Marty?"

"It sounds farfetched, I know. Marty didn't seem too concerned about it when I suggested it." She shook her head. "Part of me really wants to think it was just an accident, a coincidence that it happened at a place that was full of people from the rodeo."

"But we both know that coincidences like that don't

happen often. Doesn't the Quinn Sense tell you anything?"

"No, only that Marty is in some kind of danger. I tried to warn him, but he's not taking me seriously, and I can't blame him. I can't give him any good reason why I think he's in harm's way."

"Hmm. Tough one. Guess we'll just have to hope he'll listen to you enough to be on guard."

"I hope so."

Stephanie yawned. "I've got to get to bed. I'm dead on my feet. See you tomorrow. Don't forget to give my condolences to Seth's wife. Better yet, get her address for me, and I'll send her a card."

Clara promised to do so and clicked off her phone. She wasn't looking forward to visiting Grace Ferguson. Talking to a woman who had just lost her husband was hard. It wasn't the first time she'd done that, and she remembered how it felt to see a heartbroken widow suffering from her loss.

She dreamed that night that she was being chased around the rodeo arena by at least a dozen trucks. Rick was in the dream, calling out to her, but no matter how fast she ran toward him, he remained out of reach.

She woke up, sweating, to find Tatters' warm back pressed against hers. A glance at her clock on the bedside table assured her she'd woken up early, and she reached out a hand to turn off the alarm.

Jessie was quiet throughout breakfast, and Clara guessed

her mother was having the same qualms she was about seeing the grieving widow. When Jessie got up to call her friend, Clara took the dishes into the kitchen and stacked them in the dishwasher. She could hear her mother's low voice in the living room, but couldn't hear what was said.

Jessie walked into the kitchen as Clara was pouring detergent into the dishwasher cup. "I talked to Grace," she said, her voice not quite steady. "She said she's not very good company right now but if we want to stop by she'll be happy to see us."

"Great. What can we take her?"

"If it were me I'd want a bottle of scotch, but I guess that wouldn't look too good. Flowers?"

Clara thought for a moment. "I don't know. Flowers are more for the funeral home. How about we take her some kind of food? She probably doesn't feel like cooking."

"Or eating, if she's anything like I was when your father died." Jessie sighed. "I still remember that day as plain as if it were yesterday."

A stab of pain hit Clara under the ribs. "Me, too." She put an arm about her mother's shoulders. "This will be hard for you."

"Not as hard as it will be for Grace. Come on. Let's get it over with. We'll stop by the store first and see what we can find to take with us."

In the end they decided on ham and cheese sandwiches, a plate of fresh fruit and a large tub of ice cream.

Nancy answered the door and looked relieved when she saw them. The teenager's face was streaked with recent tears, and she wore no makeup. "Thanks for coming," she said, as she let them into the house. "Mom's in the living room. She's a mess, so be prepared. She really needs someone to talk to right now."

"Don't worry," Jessie said, giving the girl a hug. "We'll do our best to help."

There wasn't a lot they could do to help a heartbroken widow, Clara thought uneasily as she followed her mother into the living room.

Nancy had disappeared, obviously unwilling to be part of what was likely to be a painful conversation.

A familiar-looking woman sat in a chair by a large window that overlooked a shady yard. Her white face had been ravaged by shock, grief and tears, but her short, dark hair was neatly combed and she wore a spotless cream shirt over khaki pants.

Through the window Clara could see maple trees spreading thick, leafy branches over a lawn edged with hydrangea shrubs, rose bushes and a myriad of colorful annuals. Obviously someone in the Ferguson family was an avid gardener.

"My dear Grace!" Jessie rushed over to the frail-looking woman and smothered her with her arms. "I'm so terribly sorry. If there's anything we can do . . ."

Grace appeared to be fighting tears, though she managed a weak smile. "Thank you, but we'll be fine. It's just—" She swallowed, obviously unable to finish the sentence.

"Well," Jessie said briskly, "we brought you some sandwiches and fruit for lunch." She gestured at Clara, who still carried the bag of groceries. "Take them into the kitchen and put the ice cream in the freezer before it melts."

"That's very kind of you, but—" Grace began, but Jessie cut her off.

"You're entirely welcome. I know what it's like to lose someone you love. The shock, you know. It totally wipes out everything in your mind. You need to eat. It will keep your strength up." She glanced at Clara again. "You've met my daughter, Clara?"

Grace stared at Clara. Her voice sounded dull, as if she were reciting a boring poem. "You work in the bookstore on Main Street."

Clara nodded. "The Raven's Nest. I've seen you in there a couple of times. My cousin, Stephanie, owns the store. She sends her condolences, by the way. We knew Seth quite well. He used to come in a lot. He was one of our best customers."

Grace nodded, her voice thickening. "He loved science fiction, especially books about the future. He always said he wanted to have his body frozen so he could be brought back to life in the future to see what it was like." Her voice broke on the last word. "Guess he'll never know, now."

Jessie cleared her throat. "Clara hasn't been here that long. She was living in New York until a year or so ago.

Goodness knows why she came back to Finn's Harbor, but I'm very glad she did." She frowned. "The groceries, Clara?" She nudged her head at the kitchen behind her.

Trying not to bristle at her mother's commanding tone, Clara carried the bag into the kitchen. The freezer was crammed with plastic containers of what looked like casseroles, and three tubs of ice cream. She managed to squeeze her tub on top of them and put the rest of the groceries into an already crowded fridge. Apparently Grace's neighbors had been generous with their offerings.

When she returned to the living room, her mother was seated next to Grace, talking earnestly in her ear. She stopped abruptly when Clara entered the room, leaving her no doubt that Jessie had been talking about her.

"Ah, there you are." Jessie gave her a broad smile. "I was just telling Grace what a blessing it is to have you living with me. After David died I was so terribly lonely, and now I have my daughter and an adorable dog to keep me company."

Tatters would appreciate that, Clara thought, biting her tongue. Jessie never missed an opportunity to criticize the dog, yet there was no doubt in Clara's mind that her mother adored the unpredictable animal.

"Anyway," Jessie said, turning back to Grace, "as I was saying, it's a good thing you have your daughter living with you. She'll be a great comfort in the next few months, until you get used to the idea of living without your husband."

Clara winced at the agonized shadow that crossed Grace's face. Jessie was not known for her tact, but sometimes even she went too far. Deciding it was time to jump in, she said quickly, "We were so sorry to hear about the accident. I hope the police find whoever did it. I can't believe the driver of that truck didn't stop."

Grace's face crumpled. "It was my fault," she said, covering her face with her hands. "I sent him to his death. May God forgive me, my husband died because of me."

After a shocked pause, Jessie found her voice first. "Nonsense," she said, sounding a little uncertain. "It was an accident. No one could have known that would happen."

Grace shook her head. "He wouldn't have been at that bar at all if it wasn't for me. We had a fight that night and he stormed out of here. I had no idea where he was going. He must have gone to the pub to drown his sorrows or something. He probably got drunk and never saw that truck coming."

For once Jessie seemed speechless.

Clara sat down on the other side of the weeping woman and put an arm about her shoulders. "It wasn't your fault. It could have happened anywhere, anytime."

Grace made an effort to control her sobs. Hunting in the pocket of her pants, she pulled out a wad of tissues and blew her nose. She dabbed at her eyes, muttering, "It was that lousy rodeo that started it all. I wish it had never come to town."

Stunned by the widow's words, Clara dropped her arm. "The rodeo? What does that have to do with anything?"

Jessie held up her hand. "Maybe Grace doesn't want to talk about it right now."

Grace shook her head. "No, it's all right. It will be good to talk about it. I haven't been able to say anything to Nancy about it. She gets so upset." She took a shuddering breath. "Seth wanted to go to the rodeo the first night it opened. He knew I wouldn't want to go, so he went on his own. I wasn't happy about it."

"That he went without you?" Jessie asked, with a hint of disapproval.

"That he went at all." Grace turned to the window, her face lined with pain. "He knew how much I hated the rodeo. My father died in one after being gored by a bull. I saw the whole thing. I was seven years old, and it took years to get that image out of my mind. Even now . . ." she shuddered, obviously reliving the memory.

"I'm so sorry," Clara said. "I shouldn't have asked."

"No, it's okay." Grace wiped another tear from her eyes. "When I met Seth, he was a rodeo clown. He was one of those guys who distract the bulls so they won't attack the riders."

Clara barely heard the last words. *Seth had been a rodeo clown.* She replayed her vision in her mind. She saw the parking lot again, and the clown being tossed through the air like a bean bag. So that was what the Sense had been trying to tell her. It was Seth Ferguson who'd been in danger that night. But how was she supposed to know that? Until this moment she'd had no idea Seth was remotely connected to the rodeo.

Did that mean that Seth's death was no accident, after all? He was at the rodeo the night of the murder. Had he seen something, or heard something incriminating? Had he been silenced because he knew the identity of Lisa's killer?

All at once Seth's death had become far more significant than she had imagined. If she was right, then there were now two murders to solve.

8

"Clara?"

Clara blinked, realizing that both women were staring at her. "I'm sorry. What did you say?"

She directed the question at Grace, though she was fully aware of her mother's gaze boring into her head.

"I just asked if you'd been to the rodeo," Grace said. "If so, you must have seen the bullfighters. It's what they call the clowns who distract the bulls."

"Yes, I did see them." Clara suppressed a shiver. "It scared me to watch them."

"Then you can understand how I felt when I met Seth. I fell in love with him almost at first sight. I tried to put him out of my mind. I knew there was no way I could ever have a meaningful relationship with a bullfighter, not after watching my dad die that way. But I guess you can't always control what your heart wants."

Clara almost smiled at that. She knew, only too well, what it was to listen to her heart instead of her head.

"Anyway," Grace went on, "I begged Seth to give up the rodeo. It took a while, but when he proposed and I told him I wouldn't marry him unless he gave it up, he finally agreed. Maybe it helped that the very next night he had a close call with a bull. That's when he decided he was going to invest all his savings in boating supplies." She hiccupped, and it turned into a sob. "I still can't believe he's gone."

Jessie leaned forward. "Perhaps we should go. Can we get you anything?"

"Oh, goodness. I'm so sorry." Grace started to get up. "I should have offered—"

"No need." Jessie halted her with a swift gesture of her hand. "We're just about to leave." She looked at Clara. "Aren't we, Clara?"

"Yes, in a moment." Clara looked at Grace, who had sunk back in her chair. She just had to know the rest of the story. "So what happened at the rodeo?"

A shadow crossed Grace's face. "Nothing, as far as I know. Seth came home late. I was already in bed. He didn't say much, probably because he knew I wouldn't want to talk about it. He smelled of the rodeo." She shivered. "Like he did when I first met him. How I hate that smell. He must have been hanging out with the bullfighters. He knows most of them. Anyway, he went off to work the next morning and I decided to do the laundry. That's when I found the money."

Jessie looked startled. "Money?"

"A big wad of cash. It was tucked into his jeans pocket. He'd hung them up to wear them again but I wanted to wash them. I needed to get that smell out of his clothes. When he came home I asked him about the cash. He wouldn't tell me where it came from. I got worried. I figured he'd started gambling or something."

"Seth? Gambling?" Jessie shook her head. "No, I can't believe that. He was too down-to-earth to get caught up in that mess."

Grace's face creased in pain. "I thought so too, but I know the store wasn't doing so well. He had a lot of overhead, and he was worried about the bills. I thought he might have done something crazy to get some extra cash. We ended up yelling at each other, and he stormed out." She shuddered. "That was the last time I saw him. The police called me later that night with the news."

"So you never found out where the cash came from?" Clara asked, earning a stern shake of the head from Jessie.

Tears rolled down Grace's cheeks. "No. I should have just let things be. Seth would have told me eventually. If I hadn't nagged him he wouldn't have left, and . . ." Once more she broke down in heart-wrenching sobs.

This time Jessie jumped to her feet and hugged the woman's shaking shoulders. "You can't blame yourself for what happened. You didn't tell him to leave. He left of his own accord. It was that drunk's fault. That sleazebag who didn't even stop to see if Seth was okay. He's the one to blame. Not you."

"I wish I *could* stop blaming myself." Grace turned a tearstained face up to Jessie. "Thank you for coming. And for the groceries. I really appreciate it."

It was a dismissal, and Clara stood up. "Please let us know if there's anything we can do. Or if you just want to talk."

"Yes, of course," Jessie added, giving the widow one more hug. "I'll call in a day or two to see how you're doing. Let us know when and where the funeral will be held. We'll be there."

Following her mother out of the house, Clara thought about Grace's story and wished she knew the truth about Seth's death. If it wasn't for her pesky visions, she would have had no trouble accepting it as an accident.

She just couldn't rid herself of the feeling that somehow it was all connected. But she couldn't imagine how. Maybe if she had the answer to that, she'd be closer to finding Lisa Warren's killer.

Arriving at the bookstore later that morning, she was surprised to see a long line of customers waiting to be served. Joining Stephanie behind the counter, she studied her cousin's flushed face. "What'd you do? Advertise on TV?"

"No, it's a new book by Andrea Garnett. You know, she writes about angels who help women get back the lives they thought they'd lost forever. Great series."

"Oh, right." Clara threw her purse down on the shelf and smiled at the next customer in line. "Can I help you?"

The woman thrust two books at her. "When are you going to get her here for a book signing?" she demanded.

The cousins exchanged glances. "We haven't actually thought about book signings," Stephanie began, "but—"

"Well, why not? All decent bookstores have book signings."

"Yeah," a teenaged youth said from farther down the line. "How about having George R. R. Martin in here to sign books?"

Some murmurs of "Cool!" answered him.

"I guess we need to have a book signing," Stephanie muttered.

"I'll get Molly on it next week." Clara smiled at the customer as she handed her the bagged books. "We'll see what we can do. We'll put a poster in the window when we get a signing set up."

Apparently satisfied with that, the customer left, and the cousins were kept busy with the rest of the line. An hour later, the last of the customers had been rung up, giving them some breathing space before the next onslaught.

"Wow," Stephanie said, plopping down on the couch in the Reading Nook, "that woman's series is going ballistic." She looked up at Clara. "Do you think she'd come and sign books for us?"

"I guess the only way to find out is to ask her." Clara glanced at her watch. "Shouldn't you be getting home? George will be going nuts trying to watch your three hellions."

Stephanie made a face. "Only Michael and Olivia are hellions. I barely know Ethan is in the house. He's always shut away in his room on the computer, or in the den playing video games. Sometimes I wonder who the stranger is at the dinner table."

Clara grinned. "Well, your other two make up for it."

"You can say that again." Stephanie got up. "But you're right. I'd better get home. Before I do, though, we need to move those boxes of returns. They're blocking the shelves behind them and I want to clear those off so we have room for more books."

"Isn't that where we keep the Halloween and Christmas decorations?"

"Yes, but since we only use them once a year, I thought I'd put them in the shed out back. We have plenty of room in there for them, and that will give us more shelves for books in the stockroom."

Clara shook her head. "You do like to make work for yourself."

"You know me. Have to keep busy." Stephanie was walking toward the stockroom as she spoke. "Come on. It won't take a minute to move those boxes."

Following her, Clara gave up her vision of a leisurely break in the Reading Nook before the next round of customers arrived.

It actually took closer to fifteen minutes to get the stack of boxes moved. They were down to the last half dozen or so when a soft sound made them both pause.

Clara exchanged a startled glance with her cousin. "Did you hear that?"

"I did." Stephanie stared at the boxes. "It sounded as if it came from them."

Clara backed away. "I've heard that sound before. I think it might be a rat."

Stephanie squeaked. "I hate rats!"

"Have you ever seen one?"

"No, but I know what they look like." She stared fearfully at the boxes. "They bite, don't they?"

"Only if they get the chance." Clara looked around for the broom, and found it propped up by the back door. "Okay, you move the boxes, and I'll get ready to sweep it out the door." With her free hand, she opened the door.

Stephanie looked at the boxes again. "Why don't you move them and I'll do the sweeping."

"You really want to do that?" Clara held out the broom. "Go ahead."

"Wait!" Stephanie's panicked gaze swung back and forth between the broom and the boxes. "Can't we just call an exterminator or something?"

"We could, but—" Clara broke off as another sound interrupted her—a sound she recognized. "That," she said carefully, "is no rat."

"It sounded like a cat," Stephanie said, her voice shaking just a bit.

"It did." Clara took down the top box and peered over the stack. "And it is."

Stephanie's gasp sounded more like relief than surprise. "Where? Let me look." She leaned over the stack of boxes. "How in the world—?"

Clara stared at the striped face of the tabby cat looking up at her. It seemed perfectly comfortable sitting in a box lined with a pink blanket and a navy blue shawl that Clara recognized. Nearby was a litterbox, a bowl of milk and a saucer of half-eaten cat food. "I think," she said, trying to keep the amusement out of her voice, "that you need to talk to Molly."

"Molly?" Stephanie's voice was a squeak. "Molly's keeping a cat here?"

"Well, that's Molly's shawl. She wore it a couple of times last winter when we were having all that trouble with the furnace. She hated it. She said it made her feel like a granny."

Stephanie rolled her eyes. "So she gives it to a cat?

And brings it in our store? Doesn't she know I have allergies?"

"You don't have allergies and you don't know for sure that Molly is responsible for the cat, although I don't think he set all this up for himself."

"Well, we'll soon find out." Stephanie glanced at the cat again as she pulled her phone from her pocket. "Poor thing. It's been trapped behind these boxes all this time. Why would she imprison it like that?"

"So it wouldn't come out into the store and then we'd find out about it?"

"Oh, right." Stephanie thumbed a number, then held the phone to her ear. "Molly? How are you doing?" She paused, obviously listening to Molly's answer. "Oh, that's too bad. So you still don't feel like coming out with us tonight? Okay. Well, I hope you feel better soon. By the way, guess what we just found in the stockroom."

Clara listened to the one-sided conversation with amusement, while Stephanie relayed the important points. Apparently Molly had seen the cat wandering the street on a bitterly cold night and taken pity on it. She'd fed it and left it on the doorstep of the bookstore, but the next night she'd seen it again. After the third night she'd taken it into the stockroom. Since she wasn't allowed pets in her apartment, and Clara had Tatters, and Stephanie had allergies, or at least her kids had allergies, Molly was afraid that if she told the cousins about the cat, they'd insist on taking it to a shelter. So she kept it hidden and took care of it as best she could.

"She's crying," Stephanie said, holding out the phone to Clara. "She doesn't want Edgar to go to the shelter."

"Edgar?" Clara smiled as she took the phone from her cousin. "Molly? Hold on a minute." She looked at Stephanie. "She calls the cat Edgar?"

Stephanie nodded. "After Edgar Allan Poe. She has good taste in names."

"Well," Clara said carefully, "we can't possibly take a cat named Edgar to a shelter. Why don't we just let him stay here, since he's obviously feeling at home? He won't be any trouble. Cats are very independent creatures."

"What about my allergies?"

"You don't have allergies."

Stephanie sighed. "Oh, all right. But I don't want him wandering around getting under customers' feet."

Clara spoke into the phone. "Did you hear all that, Molly?"

Molly was still sniffling. "Thanks so much, Clara. I'll take care of Edgar, I promise. Would you mind giving him some fresh milk until I get back? It's in the fridge, and his cat food is in the broom closet behind the box of cleaners."

"Don't worry. I'll see to him." Clara hung up and handed the phone back to her cousin. "Guess the Raven's Nest bookstore now has a resident cat named Edgar. At least we shouldn't have to worry about rats and mice anymore."

Stephanie brightened. "There's that. But for heaven's sake, don't bring that hound of yours into the store. He causes enough chaos when he's around. Can you imagine what would happen if he caught sight of Edgar?"

Clara could, and shuddered. "Point taken. Now why don't you get on home? I'll take care of the rest of this."

"Yeah, I'd better run. Especially since we're going out for dinner tonight. I'm really looking forward to that. Too bad Molly's going to miss it." She got to the door and looked back. "By the way, how did the visit with Seth's wife go? Was it real bad?"

"No, not really." Clara frowned, recalling Grace's words. "I guess the Sense did warn me about the accident, after all. I just didn't realize it meant Seth." She repeated most of the story Grace had told her.

"Whoa," Stephanie murmured, when Clara was finished. "That's so weird. Why would you see Marty in the vision instead of Seth?"

"I have no idea. Anyway, we can't worry about that now. We need to concentrate on finding out who killed Lisa."

Stephanie shook her head. "If Dan doesn't know by now, how are we going to find out who did it?"

"There's still the vision I had of the person in the red shirt. I actually saw the killer, Steffie. I just wish I could see his face."

"Maybe you'll have the vision again."

"Maybe. Though unless he turns around I still won't see his face."

"You still think it's Wes, don't you?"

"I know that Dan thinks Wes is the killer. He's just having trouble proving it. I wish I could help, but the only clue I have right now is the vision that I can't tell him about."

"What about Anita? She had Wes's red shirt for a while."

"She gave it back to him before the murder, remember? He was wearing it that night."

"Oh, yeah. Frustrating." Stephanie opened the door. "Maybe we'll find out tonight that Paul Eastcott was lying about being at the restaurant. That would make him a suspect, right?"

"I guess." Clara waved good-bye, feeling disgruntled. She would love to clear Wes's name, since it meant so much to Rick, but she couldn't ignore the fact that Wes had three strikes against him—the pigging string, his stormy relationship with Lisa and the red shirt. If Paul's alibi held up, they would be back to square one.

She spent the rest of the afternoon trying to put the murder out of her mind. A steady stream of customers helped her do that, and late in the day things brightened up considerably when she saw Rick's tall figure appear in the doorway.

"I came to see if you've heard about Seth Ferguson,"

he said, as she led him down the aisle to the Reading Nook.

"Yes, I did. I still can't believe it." She picked up the coffeepot. "Want some? It's been sitting a while."

He shook his head. "The weird thing is, Wes told me yesterday afternoon when he was in the shop that an old buddy of his had been killed in a hit-and-run. I didn't realize at the time that it was Seth. Not until I saw it on the news last night."

Remembering Grace's words, Clara nodded. "I visited Seth's wife this morning. She said Seth used to be a rodeo clown, and knew most of the guys in the rodeo."

"Yeah, I guess the news was all over the rodeo the next morning. It must have been a shock to them. Wes told me they were all talking to Seth in the pub minutes before he went outside and got run down."

"How awful." The memory of her vision was still fresh in her mind, and she shivered. "Two deaths in two days. You know what they say about threes."

Rick wound an arm across her shoulders. "I do, and I know it's just a fallacy, so quit your worrying. Go out tonight and have a good time. Put all this out of your mind."

"I'll try." She watched him leave, wishing she could forget the visions that haunted her.

By the time the last customer had left, Edgar had taken up residence on the counter. His presence was strangely comforting as he watched her enter the last of the receipts in the computer. After giving him some fresh milk from the fridge, she found the cans of food in the broom closet and opened up a can for him.

"There you go, Edgar," she said, watching the cat curl up in his bed. "Sleep well and keep your eyes open for mice, okay?"

She was at the door when the voice spoke in her head. *No problem.*

Startled, she looked back at the cat. He stared back at her, his eyes gleaming gold in the reflection from the light overhead.

Wonderful. Now she was reading the cat's thoughts. Shaking her head, she gently closed the door and locked it.

The Pioneer Inn was crowded when the cousins arrived there later. Clara had expected something rustic and a little primitive, in keeping with the restaurant's name. She was pleasantly surprised to see an elegant dining room with a nautical theme. Old-fashioned lanterns hung on the walls above the tables, and mother-of-pearl sea-shells provided bases for candles.

Boats and lighthouses decorated the wallpaper, and tiny blue anchors were embroidered on the corners of the white tablecloths.

The restaurant was noted for its seafood, so Clara ordered the salmon, while Stephanie chose the coconut shrimp. The waiters wore a mock naval uniform, and the guy who waited on them seemed somewhat stuffy at first, but after Stephanie worked her magic on him, he softened up a bit.

"When are you going to ask him about Paul?" Stephanie asked, watching the waiter as he strode back to the kitchen. "What if he wants to know why you're asking?"

Clara poked her fork into her salmon. "I'll tell him we have a bet. You say Paul was at the rodeo that night, I say he was here."

Stephanie frowned. "That's a bit lame, isn't it?"

Clara finished her mouthful of fish before answering. "I know, but I couldn't think of anything else. I'm hoping it won't get that far. I'm hoping he'll take one look at the picture and say, 'Oh, right. He was just here the other night.' Then that will take care of it."

Her mouth full, Stephanie nodded. "That would help a lot," she said, when she could speak again.

Clara grinned. "This salmon is delicious. It was worth the trip for the food."

"And the wine." Stephanie took a sip of hers. "We should do this more often. Preferably when we're not investigating a murder."

"Shhh!" Clara glanced at the next table, but the couple who sat there were too engrossed in each other to pay attention to anything else. "Let's change the subject. Tell me how the kids are doing."

It was the right thing to ask her cousin, who launched into a string of tales about the latest escapades of her offspring. "They remind me so much of us when we were their age," she said, as she laid her fork down on her empty plate. "Do you remember when you tried to hypnotize your neighbor's dog?"

Clara rolled her eyes. "That's something I'd prefer to forget."

Stephanie started to laugh. "You kept swinging your father's pocket watch in front of his face, chanting"—she lowered her voice to a hollow drawl—" 'Sleep, you stupid dog. Go to *sleep.*' "

"What a waste of time."

"Yeah, until the dog snatched the watch and ran off with it. Then it got fun—the two of us chasing that dog all over the yard . . ."

"And across the street . . ."

"Where he dropped the watch into the ditch . . ."

"And I had to climb down in the stinging nettles to get it. I had a rash for weeks."

Still laughing, Stephanie looked up as the waiter approached, carrying a tray loaded with mouthwatering concoctions of fruit, cream and chocolate. "Ooh, that looks *so* good!" She pointed to a chocolate mousse decorated with whipped cream and a fresh strawberry.

"I'll have the crème brûlée," Clara said with a smile.

The waiter smiled back. "Good choice."

"Oh, as long as you're here"—she snatched up her purse—"I wonder if you recognize this man?" She dug out the picture she'd cut from the newspaper and held it up for him to see.

The waiter stared at the photo for a long second or two, before murmuring, "I'm sorry. I don't know him."

"He's the project manager at the new Hill Top Resort out on the coast road," Stephanie said helpfully. "You know, the one with the golf course and everything?"

The waiter gave her a blank look. "The Hill Top? Sorry, I don't know it. I'll be back directly with your desserts." He sailed off to pause at another table with his tray.

Stephanie frowned. "He must have heard of the Hill Top," she said, staring at the waiter's back. "It's been all over the news for months."

Clara sat back in her seat. "He was lying," she said quietly.

Stephanie stared at her. "He was? How do you . . . well, of course you know. The Sense told you, right?"

"Right." She leaned forward again. "What I'd like to know is what he was lying about—Paul being here, or knowing about the Hill Top."

Stephanie puffed out her breath. "Maybe he just didn't want to answer what could be awkward questions. In any case, that still doesn't tell us whether or not Paul was here that night."

Clara looked around. "We'll have to ask someone else. The woman who seated us. She'd probably remember him if he was here."

"Good thinking." The waiter returned with their selections, and Stephanie dug into her dessert. "Now let's enjoy these gorgeous treats and forget they're full of calories."

The moment they were finished and had signed the bill, Clara stood up. "Come on, let's go ask that woman if she recognizes Paul."

Reluctantly, Stephanie followed her, murmuring, "I could get used to living like this."

Out in the foyer, the woman who had seated them greeted them both. "I hope you enjoyed your meal?"

"It was great," Clara assured her. "We'll be sure to come back again."

"That's good to hear." The woman walked over to the door to open it for them. She wore a tight black skirt that barely covered her thighs and a white blouse. Her dark hair was caught up at the back of her head with a gold comb, and when she turned to them again, her smile revealed dazzling white teeth. "Thank you for coming."

Clara slipped the newspaper cutting out of her purse and held it out to her. "We were wondering if you've ever seen this man in here."

The woman took the photo and studied it. "I'm sorry. I don't recognize him." She turned to another woman who had just entered the foyer, dressed in the same black skirt and white blouse. "Stacey? Have you seen this man in here?"

Stacey sauntered over to look at the photo. "Nope, not that I can remember."

"Well, thank you," Clara said, tucking the photo back into her purse. She stepped outside and waited for Stephanie to join her.

"Well, that went well." Stephanie jerked her head at the door. "Were they lying, too?"

"I don't know." Clara headed down the steps and across the parking lot to her car. "They could have a code or something that prevents them from talking about their customers. If that's so, we still don't know for sure if Paul was here the night of the murder. If everyone in there was lying to protect him, all they managed to do was prevent him from proving his alibi."

"Unless they weren't lying, and Paul was never here."

"I guess there's no way we can really know at this point."

"This is getting very complicated."

"Tell me about it." Clara pressed the unlock button on her key chain, and a slight beep answered her. Once she was seated in the car, she waited for Stephanie to climb in next to her before saying, "I know someone who might be able to tell us where Paul was that night."

Stephanie sounded tired when she answered. "Who?"

"His wife."

Her cousin's voice rose a notch. "You're going to talk to Paul's wife?"

"Paul did seem nervous when we were talking about Lisa's murder. I think he's hiding something. I need to find out what that is."

"You think his wife will tell us, even if she knows what it is?"

Clara shrugged. "Probably not, but maybe the Sense will."

Stephanie shook her head. "When has the Sense ever come through when you need it?"

"True, but it's worth a shot. If we can eliminate Paul, it will be one less suspect to worry about."

"And we'd still have no idea who did it."

Clara started the engine, staring gloomily through the windshield. "We're not very good at this."

"We're doing our best. We're not exactly private eyes, and it might help to remember nobody is paying us to do this. Not only that, the cops aren't happy with us sticking our noses in where they don't belong. I'd say we're pretty much on our own here, so if we mess up, nobody can blame us."

"Except I feel I'm letting Rick down."

"He can't expect you to do any more than you're doing."

Clara pulled out onto the road. "He doesn't. In fact, he told me he doesn't want us getting too involved. At the same time, he really cares about Wes, and if Wes is innocent, there's nothing I'd rather do than prove it."

"Okay, then. Let's move on to Mrs. Eastcott, and hope the Sense comes through for you this time. Do you know where they live?"

"No, but it shouldn't be that hard to figure out. You can find just about anything on the Web."

Stephanie sighed. "I know. It's scary." Her voice tightened. "Something just occurred to me. What happens if you have a vision while you're driving?"

Clara gave her a grim smile. "Let's hope we never have to find out."

9

Sunday was always a short day at the Raven's Nest, since the bookstore opened at noon and closed at five. It seemed longer to Clara, however, because she worked the day alone. There were fewer tourists in town, as most of them were either leaving or arriving, and the regulars rarely visited the store on a Sunday.

She was therefore happy, though somewhat surprised, to see Tim Rossi in the doorway that Sunday afternoon. "What are you doing here?" she asked, as he strolled over to the counter. "I thought you'd be off fishing in that boat of yours."

Tim shook his head, his usual smile barely visible. "I didn't feel like going, after what happened to Seth. He outfitted the boat for me when I bought it. It feels like a sacrilege to be out enjoying myself in it when he's lying in a funeral home."

"I'm sorry." Clara sobered at once. "I know you and Seth were close."

"We were." Tim tapped the counter with his fingers. "I just wish we could find the creep who ran him down. I'd fling his ass in jail and let him rot there."

"Still no clue, huh?"

"None."

"What about the rodeo murder? Any progress with that?"

Tim shook his head. "It's tough. We've tried talking to the rodeo folk, but they're a tight-knit group and seem afraid of getting someone in trouble. Nobody's talking, and without their help, we're getting nowhere. Dan still thinks Wes Carlton is the perp, but without proof we can't hold him. The rodeo leaves town on Tuesday morning. We can't make them stay, and once they're gone, it seems unlikely we'll ever solve the murder."

Clara fought the urge to tell Tim about her conversation with Paul Eastcott. After all, she had nothing much to add to what the police already knew, and Dan would not be happy to hear she'd been snooping again. "So you're certain someone connected to the rodeo killed Lisa, then?"

Tim shrugged. "It looks that way, considering she was strangled with a pigging string."

"But anyone could have found it lying on the ground."

"Not likely. From what the cowboys told me, a calf-roper's pigging string is as important to him as his saddle. He's not going to leave it lying around somewhere. No, Dan's convinced it's an inside job and Carlton is our man." He glanced at the clock, as if realizing he'd been saying too much. "I'd better get down to the Nook. I hope there's still a Danish left?"

"A whole plateful. It's been quiet this morning."

Grinning, he gave her a nod and disappeared down the aisle.

She was just thinking about joining him when the door opened, jingling the bell above it. Looking up, Clara saw John Halloran heading her way and smothered a sigh. Whenever John visited the store, things tended to get complicated.

"It's hot out there," John grumbled, when he paused at the counter. "It's not even summer yet."

"Not far off," Clara said cheerfully. "What can I do for you, John?"

He glared at Edgar, who was sitting on the counter, cleaning his paw with his tongue. "What's *that* doing there?"

"That," Clara said, holding on to her smile, "is Edgar. He lives here now."

John sniffed. "Not very hygienic, having a cat lying around on the counter."

"We're not serving food up here." Clara reached out

to smooth Edgar's ruffled fur. "He's not allowed in the Nook."

"Good thing too, or I'd be forced to report you."

Edgar stretched his neck. *Jerk.*

"Were you looking for something specific?" Clara asked hastily.

"I ordered the first book in the Knights of Wisdom series. Is it in yet?" John stared around the store as if expecting the book to jump out at him.

"Not yet, I'm afraid."

John shot her a look that would have stopped a raging bull in its tracks. "Why not? I've waited way too long for it already, thanks to your incompetent cousin losing my order."

"We just ordered it again this week. We're waiting for the next delivery."

Scowling, John stuck his hands in the pockets of his Dockers.

The pants looked like they needed a washing, and Clara felt a pang of sympathy for the man. He lived alone, having been divorced from his wife after he lost the Sweet Spot, a candy store he used to own farther down the hill.

Clara and Stephanie had visited his store often when they were kids, and were convinced that John was an evil wizard. He was always threatening them with dire consequences if they touched any of his candy without buying it. With his bushy hair and eyebrows, and fierce brown eyes glaring at them through the dark-rimmed glasses perched on his nose, he'd seemed formidable and, at times, downright menacing.

The girls never went into his store alone, and once there had bought their candy and fled before he could change them into frogs—or something much worse.

Even now, when John looked at her a certain way and spoke in his low, creepy voice, Clara got chills and couldn't wait to get him out of the bookstore.

Trying to think of a book that might interest him, she tapped the keyboard to bring up the latest deliveries on the computer. "We have a couple of new sci-fi thrillers that came in last week. Would you like to see them?"

John gave her one of his drop-dead looks. "Give me the titles. I'll find them on the shelves."

She quickly scribbled down the titles and handed them to him. "They're halfway down the second aisle."

"I know where to look." He turned away, then seemed to have a thought. Turning back, he asked abruptly, "I guess you heard about Seth Ferguson."

Clara nodded. "I did. It's so sad."

"Yeah. I just saw him the night before he died. Hard to believe he's gone." Shaking his head, he turned away again.

Obeying an impulse, Clara asked quickly, "Where did you see him?"

John paused, his back toward her, as if reluctant to answer. Finally, he looked at her over his shoulder. "He was shutting up shop as I was walking by. It was around six. I asked him why he was closing early. He said he was going to the rodeo."

It was on the tip of Clara's tongue to tell John that Seth used to compete in the rodeo, but for some reason, she felt reluctant to share that bit of knowledge with him.

"I was going to ask him what the heck he saw in that rowdy, messy show," John went on, "but he had someone else with him, and he shot off like he didn't want to talk about it."

Probably because he knew his wife wouldn't approve, Clara thought, remembering Grace's story. A thought occurred to her, and she asked carefully, "Who was with him? A woman?"

John's look of disgust quickly told her she was wrong. "What's wrong with you people, jumping to conclusions all the time? No, it wasn't a woman. It was a man, and by the looks of him he had a belly full of beer." He wandered off, muttering to himself.

Clara watched him disappear down the aisle, wondering who was with Seth that night, and whether he'd still be alive had he not decided to go to the rodeo without his wife.

In the next instant she was no longer in the bookstore.

She was at the rodeo, but she seemed to be completely alone—no cheering crowds in the seats, no cowboys chasing calves, not a sign of movement anywhere. The night sky twinkled with stars overhead, and beyond the arena, darkness shrouded the landscape.

Clara glanced at the steps, afraid she would see Marty toppling down them. All she could see was the dust stirred by the wind, and a single piece of paper fluttering nearby. She reached for it, but it slipped out of her fingers. As it floated away she could see Marty's eyes staring at her and realized it had been torn from a rodeo poster.

A movement caught her eye, and she looked back at the arena. A clown was jogging toward the chutes. At first she thought it was Marty, but this clown wore a bright blue suit, and his face was painted blue and red. He wore no hat, and his bright red wig gleamed in the overhead lights.

When he reached the middle of the arena he paused, his head on one side as if he were listening. Then she heard it—the scraping of hoofs and the snorting of fiery nostrils.

The clown looked up at her, his hands outstretched as if pleading with her. Without warning the bull burst from the chutes, heading straight for the clown.

Clara surged to her feet. She tried to shout but her voice was no louder than a whisper. Frantically beckoning with her arms, she raced down the steps.

The clown seemed unaware of the bull bearing down on him. He pushed his hands in her direction, as if commanding her to stay away.

Her legs felt weak, and no matter how hard she ran, she couldn't seem to get any closer. Again she tried to shout a warning, but the wind snatched the words from her mouth. She felt a desperate sense of helplessness as the bull drew close, and she closed her eyes, unable to watch the horrific scene unfolding in front of her.

"You really need to do something about that indigestion."

Clara snapped her eyes open to find herself back in the Raven's Nest, with Rick standing on the other side of the counter, his face creased in concern. She swallowed, forced a smile and said unsteadily, "I'll take some antacids."

"Good idea." He moved closer. "Seriously, you might want to check things out with your doctor. You look a bit fragile."

She actually managed a light laugh. "No one's ever called me that before."

He grinned back at her, though his eyes still held a trace of anxiety. "Is everything okay at home?"

Feeling guilty for worrying him, she walked around the counter and slipped a hand through his arm. "Couldn't be better. Why don't you come and see for yourself?"

He wrapped an arm around her, pulling her close. "Are you inviting me to your house?"

She hadn't meant that at all, but now that the words were out there, she didn't know how to take them back. "Come to dinner," she said, hoping she wasn't making one huge mistake. "My mother has been panting to meet you."

"Oh, we already met. She came into the store."

Shocked, Clara drew back to look at him. "You're kidding. She never said anything to me."

"Charming woman." He looked as if he were enjoying surprising her. "She thinks the world of you."

Clara was getting an uncomfortable feeling in her stomach. "What did she say about me?"

"Only that you're really smart, and she can't understand why you gave up a promising career as a literature professor to live here in Finn's Harbor and work in a bookstore." He gave her a long look. "I take it she still doesn't know about what happened in New York."

Annoyed that her mother had been discussing her behind her back, Clara answered sharply, "No one does. You are the only person who knows what happened. I'd like to keep it that way."

There was no way she wanted her mother to know she had planned to get married in New York. She'd wanted a quiet, intimate wedding with just a couple of friends, and had figured on surprising everyone with the news afterward. As it turned out, it was just as well she hadn't told anyone.

"I know," Rick said, pulling her close again. "Trust me, I won't breathe a word to anyone else. Especially your mother. A mother would tend to overreact when her daughter was badly mistreated by a lousy jerk who didn't know what a fantastic woman he'd let get away."

Her relief made her smile. "Thank you. You obviously know my mother well."

He shook his head. "No, as a matter of fact, I only talked to her once. I meant what I said, though. She really cares about you. I could tell by the way she was sizing me up, trying to decide if I was good enough for her daughter's attention."

Clara pulled a face. "Not that she has any say in the matter. I make my own decisions."

"So now that we have that straight, does the invitation still stand? I'd like to get to know your mother so she can see what a great guy I am."

She laughed up at him. "You'd have to be a saint to impress my mother."

"As long as I impress you. That's all I care about."

"Oh, for pity's sake, get a room." John Halloran's voice swiveled both their heads in his direction. "This is supposed to be a bookstore, not a dance floor. If you want to snuggle, go find an empty car."

Clara pushed herself away from Rick. "Sorry. Did you find what you're looking for?"

"I found these." John shuffled forward and thrust two books at her. "They look decent enough. I guess they'll do until my order comes in." He gave Rick a lethal stare. "Who's looking after the hardware store, then?"

"My assistant, Tyler." Rick winked at Clara. "He's a good kid, but not as thorough as you used to be, John."

John sniffed. "Kids today don't know what work is. When I worked for you I had everything in shipshape order. I knew where everything was on the shelves and could put my hand on it in seconds. That assistant of yours couldn't tell you where the restroom is, much less any of the merchandise."

"You're right, John," Rick said solemnly. "I do miss your expertise. Anytime you want to come back and work for me, just let me know."

John grunted. "Can't stand on my feet all day anymore, or I would." He turned to Clara, who had bagged the books and was waiting for him to pay for them. "I can't hang around here talking all day, either. Got things to do." He swiped his card, waited for his receipt then left, mumbling to himself as he went out the door.

"I guess you haven't heard any more about the murder," Rick said, as the door closed behind John.

"Nothing helpful." Clara filed the copy of the receipt and entered it in the computer. "We tried to find out last night if Paul Eastcott had eaten dinner at the Pioneer Inn the night of the murder. Everyone we spoke to didn't remember seeing him, but we don't really know if they were just trying to protect their customers. So we still don't know for sure if his alibi holds up."

"He must have told the cops the same thing, and I'm sure Dan would have checked it out."

She stared at him. "I don't know why I didn't think of that. That could be why nobody wanted to tell us anything."

He gave her a long look. "So you did go there to ask questions. You're not giving up on this thing."

"Nope." She walked around the counter and laid a hand on his arm. "Don't worry, I'll be careful. I know what you went through when you were accused of murder. If Wes is innocent, I want to help clear his name."

"That means a lot to me. Wes's career is on the line. It's his whole life. I don't know what he'd do if he couldn't compete."

"I know."

"But that doesn't mean I want you risking your life to save my buddy."

"All I'm doing is asking a few questions." She grinned up at him. "Besides, with Steffie and Tatters at my side, what harm can come to me?"

He still looked worried. "Well, okay. But promise me, at the first sign of trouble, you'll get out of the way and let Dan handle it."

"I promise." She decided not to mention that she planned on talking to Diane Eastcott. If she got anything useful from Paul's wife, she'd tell him afterward.

"I see you have a new assistant." Rick nodded at Edgar, who was now snoozing with his jaw on his paws.

Clara grinned. "Meet Edgar. Molly had been hiding him in the stockroom. Steffie and I found him when we were moving boxes around."

"Ah, so that explains the scuffling sounds you heard in there."

"Right. I guess my worries about rats and mice are over as long as Edgar is around."

"He looks capable enough." He glanced at his watch. "So when should I come for dinner, and what can I bring?"

"Tuesday night? It's my day off, so I'll have plenty of time to prepare. You don't need to bring anything."

"Tuesday night it is. I'll have Tyler close up. Around seven?"

She smiled, though her stomach was churning with doubts. "Seven is fine. Tatters will be overjoyed to see you, so brace yourself."

"I'm looking forward to it." He blew her a kiss and headed for the door.

Several minutes after Rick left, Tim appeared from one of the aisles, carrying a book. Handing it to Clara, he muttered, "It's for my mom."

Hoping fervently he hadn't overheard her conversation with Rick, she took it from him and glanced at the cover. Another fantasy romance. It was the fourth book in the series he'd bought in the last month. Taking it over to the counter, she wondered if Tim was really buying the books for his mom, or if he was reading them himself.

She was sorely tempted to ask him about Paul's alibi, but that would lead to questions of how she knew about the alibi in the first place. Besides, her reasons for wanting to talk to Paul's wife went beyond the alibi thing.

If Mrs. Eastcott suspected her husband was having an affair with his assistant, that could well be a motive for murder. Clara was very anxious to meet Paul's wife to find out what kind of person she was, and if she seemed capable of killing someone.

The moment the deputy left, Clara turned to the computer and entered Paul's name in the search engine. It took only a minute or two to find his address, and she quickly wrote it down on a sticky pad and pulled off the page. Tucking it into her pocket, she left the counter and headed for the first aisle. It was time to tidy up the shelves, then close up shop.

Half an hour later she was in her car in the parking lot, her phone pressed to her ear.

Stephanie answered on the second ring. "Are you okay? Is everything all right at the store?"

Clara sighed. "Why do you always assume something is wrong when I call?"

"Because it usually is when you call."

"That's ridiculous."

"I know. Just a minute." There was a pause, then she added, "Oh, it's okay. For a minute there I thought Michael had drowned the cat, but I just saw it running out the door."

"Drowned the cat?" Clara shook her head. "Why would you think that?"

"Because he keeps saying Jasper needs a bath. I caught him in the bathroom this morning, trying to give him one in the toilet bowl."

"It's a miracle that cat survives."

"It is, indeed. So why are you calling just as I'm getting dinner?"

"I thought we could go visit Paul's wife tonight. That's if you're not busy."

"I'm always busy. What if Paul is there?"

"He won't be. He'll be at the rodeo. He's there every night according to the article I read on the local news website."

"Except for the night of Lisa's murder."

"So he says. Now's our chance to find out."

"If we're lucky. So what's our excuse for our visit?"

"The one we always use. We're doing an article."

"What kind of article?"

"I don't know." They were both silent for a moment, until Stephanie suggested, "How about an article on influential women in Finn's Harbor?"

"There's a whole bunch of articles like that on Diane Eastcott. We need to find something unique so she doesn't brush us off."

"All right, what if we tell her we're doing an article for a fashion magazine and want to feature not only her, but her home as well. I bet she'd go for that."

Relieved, Clara let out her breath. "Perfect. I'll call her and see if I can set it up for tonight. I'll call you back." She stabbed the end button and fished in her pocket for the sticky note.

Diane Eastcott answered right away. She sounded impatient at first, but when Clara explained why she was calling, Diane's tone changed. "I was planning on a quiet evening," she said. "Could we make it one night next week?"

"I'm sorry," Clara told her, "but I have a strict deadline. I just got the go-ahead from the magazine and I need to start work on it tomorrow. Of course, if you're busy, I could ask someone else—"

"On, no, don't do that." Diane hesitated, then added quickly, "I guess tonight will be okay. What time?"

Clara glanced at her watch. "Would eight p.m. work for you?"

"That will be fine. You have the address?"

After assuring her that she had all she needed, Clara hung up and hit Stephanie's speed dial.

"Did she go for it?" her cousin asked, the second she answered.

"Of course. We're expected there at eight p.m. I'll pick you up around seven thirty."

Stephanie sounded worried when she responded, "What shall we do if she asks which magazine it is?"

"We'll tell her it's for *Vogue*."

"She's going to want a copy of the article."

"We'll just have to tell her they decided not to buy it."

"What about photographers?"

"Bring your camera."

"My phone is my camera."

"I mean that big old clunker you used to wave about at parties."

"That's my father's camera, and it's almost as old as I am. It needs film, for pity's sake, and I don't have any. I don't even know if they make film like that anymore."

"Diane Eastcott won't know that. Besides, it looks authentic."

Stephanie's sigh echoed down the line. "You know we're becoming accomplished liars, don't you?"

"I know. It bothers me, too. I guess I could always submit the article to *Vogue*. They'll probably turn it down, but at least it won't be an outright lie."

"Does that mean I have to take real pictures?"

"Maybe you could take a few with your phone when she's not looking."

"This is getting so ridiculous."

"Yeah, but it's all for a good cause." Clara was smiling as she hung up, though she had to admit to a disquieting sense of guilt. She didn't like the pretense and lies any more than her cousin did, but there were times when they had no other option.

Diane Eastcott was not going to discuss her husband's whereabouts with complete strangers off the street. They had to gain her confidence and trust if they were going to learn anything useful.

Pulling out onto the street, Clara refused to acknowledge that all her hopes were pinned on the possibility that Paul Eastcott was the killer, thus clearing Wes of the crime. She had to keep an open mind if she were to get at the truth. She was running out of time, and if Wes was innocent, his career had to be saved.

If he was guilty, on the other hand, she really wanted to see him arrested before the rodeo left town. Either way, she would feel she'd done her best for Rick, though every fiber of her being prayed that Wes was not the killer. If he was, and she was the one who found the evidence that led to his arrest, that might affect her relationship with Rick. And not in a good way.

10

A little after seven thirty that evening, Clara picked up her cousin and headed for Diane Eastcott's home. She was a little startled to see Stephanie wearing a royal blue cocktail dress sparkling with crystals and a fake diamond–encrusted comb pinning up her blonde hair. "You look like you're going to a New Year's Eve party."

"Too much?" Stephanie pouted. "I was going for the professional fashion photographer look."

"It's more like a high school prom look."

"That bad?" Stephanie pulled the flap down to look in the mirror. "I could take out the comb."

"Good idea. What did George say when he saw you dressed like that?"

"He asked me who was getting married." Stephanie dragged the comb from her hair and combed the strands back into place with her fingers. "Did you tell Aunt Jessie where we're going?"

"Yeah. She wanted to come with us." Clara glanced at the camera bag sitting on her cousin's lap. "Do you remember how to work that thing?"

"It's like all cameras. You just point and click the button."

"What about focusing and all that stuff?"

"I'll fake it." Stephanie's voice wavered. "We're not going to get into trouble for this, are we?"

In spite of her tightened nerves, Clara had to laugh. "I wish I had a dollar for every time you said that when we were kids."

"So do I." Stephanie lapsed into silence, and Clara concentrated on the road as they headed into the upscale district where the Eastcotts lived. Following the directions the calm voice on her GPS gave her, she pulled up outside a pair of large iron gates, behind which a long driveway led up between perfectly manicured lawns to the stone steps of a massive house.

"Wow," Stephanie murmured, staring at it through the car window. "Paul Eastcott and his wife are living well."

"No kidding." Spying the intercom at the side of the gate, Clara stepped out of the car to press the button.

A female voice floated out through the speaker. "Who is it?"

"Clara Quinn. I have my photographer with me. We're here for our appointment."

"Come right in." The gates slid silently open, allowing Clara to drive through and up to the house.

"This is some house," Stephanie said, as they pulled up in front of the steps. "It's not surprising Paul wants to hang on to his marriage."

"Exactly." Clara cut the engine and leaned back. "It gives him a pretty strong motive for murder if he was having an affair with Lisa. Maybe she was threatening to tell his wife if he didn't ask for a divorce."

"Classic murder-mystery stuff." Stephanie opened the door and clambered out of the car. "I wish now I'd worn pants and flats. I'd forgotten how hard it is to walk in heels. Especially when I'm carrying this thing." She hauled the cumbersome camera off the backseat and slammed the door shut with her hip.

"Just slip off your shoes when you get inside the door," Clara said, as she led the way over to the steps. "Diane will thank you."

"Great idea. Thanks." Stephanie grunted as she heaved the bag up on her shoulder.

Inside the shaded porch a large pot of geraniums nodded in the breeze. Next to it, a tall, willowy, metallic Siamese cat sat staring at them with fixed golden eyes. The eyes blinked, making Clara jump. Wondering if she'd imagined it, she stepped up to the front door just as it opened. Apparently the cat was some kind of sensor.

A stern-faced woman with gray hair and glasses peered up at her. "Ms. Quinn?"

"Yes." Clara smiled. "This is my photographer, Stephanie Dowd. We have an appointment with Mrs. Eastcott."

"This way, please." After waiting for them to shed their shoes, the woman led them down a long hallway covered in maroon carpeting that embraced Clara's toes like a soft pillow under her feet.

Cream wallpaper with pale green willow trees and blue waterfalls hugged the walls, and gleaming oak doors on either side guarded the rooms. Reaching the end of the hallway, the housekeeper turned into a narrow passage and then out into a solarium, where tall glass walls overlooked a luscious lawn bordered with hydrangeas and rosebushes, and a scattering of mimosa trees.

A woman with smooth, platinum blonde hair falling about her shoulders sat in a rattan chair, staring out at the gardens. On the small table at her side ice was melting in a glass half full of water. The woman turned toward them when the housekeeper announced, in a voice heavy with disapproval, "Mrs. Eastcott, this is Ms. Quinn and Ms. Dowd."

Diane Eastcott looked as if she really did belong on the cover of *Vogue*. Her makeup was impeccable, and dressed in flowing, wide-legged brown pants and a coffee-colored silk shirt, she appeared both comfortable and incredibly chic.

Envisioning her own blue cotton pants and sleeveless

white top, Clara felt decidedly dowdy—one of her mother's favorite expressions. Holding out her hand, she advanced on Diane, her smile feeling fixed and awkward. "I'm Clara Quinn. I've looked forward to meeting you, Mrs. Eastcott. You have a lovely home."

"Thank you." Ignoring Clara's attempt at a handshake, Diane waved at another rattan chair across from her. "You can call me Diane." She ran her gaze over Stephanie, who stood gazing at the woman as if she were starstruck. "And this is?"

"My photographer, Stephanie Dowd." Clara fiercely signaled at her cousin with her eyebrows.

Stephanie appeared to make an effort to pull herself together. "Happy to meet you, Mrs. Eastcott."

"Diane." Paul's wife turned back to Clara. "I assume your photographer will want to take pictures of the house?"

"Yes, of course." Clara looked at Stephanie. "You have everything you need?"

As if suddenly realizing she was being dismissed, Stephanie looked worried. "Yes, I think so."

"Mrs. Schwartz will show you the house," Diane said, nodding at the housekeeper. "Just let her take pictures of whatever she wants. Oh, and bring me some more ice."

"Yes, Mrs. Eastcott."

"Thank you," Stephanie mumbled, with a quick, panicked look at Clara.

"This way," Mrs. Schwartz barked, and, heaving the

heavy camera higher on her shoulder, Stephanie staggered after her and out of sight.

Left alone with this icon of sophistication, what little confidence Clara was clinging to rapidly disintegrated. Reminding herself that she had done this many times before, she pulled her recorder from her pocket and sat down. "I have your permission to record our conversation?"

Diane hesitated for a second, then leaned back in her chair. "As long as you don't get too personal." She reached for the glass and swallowed a couple of mouthfuls before putting it down again.

Clara switched on the recorder and laid it on the table between them. She'd made a list of the things she wanted to ask, and she pulled it from her purse. After asking a few general questions about the house, she said casually, "I interviewed your husband a couple of days ago. He might have mentioned it. I wrote a review of the rodeo. You can find it on the city council's website."

Diane took another gulp from her glass. "Oh, that rodeo. Frankly I can't imagine why my father thinks we need rodeos to publicize the Hill Top chain. The resorts should speak for themselves."

"I take it you don't care for the rodeo?"

Diane sniffed. "I don't care for all the work it entails. My husband has been rushing around all week, missing meals at home and spending most of his time worrying about the whole thing. I can't see that it does anything for the resort, and now that dreadful girl is dead and everyone remotely connected to the rodeo is under suspicion. The whole thing is a travesty. I just wish—" She broke off as the housekeeper walked through the door carrying a pitcher of ice and a bottle.

Watching Diane refill her glass, Clara realized that the woman was drinking something a lot stronger than water.

As if reading her thoughts, Diane raised the bottle, waving it unsteadily at Clara. "Would you like a drink?"

Noting that the bottle contained gin, Clara glanced at Mrs. Schwartz, who was staring at her as if daring her to accept the offer. "Thanks, but I'm fine," she said quickly, and the housekeeper turned to leave.

"Where's the photographer?" Diane demanded, halting her at the door.

"I left her taking pictures in the bedrooms." Mrs. Schwartz's sour face turned even more forbidding. "I figured your *ice* was more important."

Her emphasis on the word clearly indicated her disapproval, and Diane's cheeks warmed. "That will be all," she said coldly.

The door snapped shut behind the housekeeper.

"It's impossible to find decent help these days." Diane stood the bottle on the table and raised the glass to her lips. "What were we talking about?"

"The rodeo." Clara leaned forward. "I was so sorry to hear about Lisa Warren's death. Your husband must be devastated."

Diane took a large gulp of the gin and coughed. "What's that supposed to mean?"

Clara hurried to reassure her. "I only meant that she was his assistant, and a very good one, according to some of the people who work with the rodeo. As you said, it's hard to find good help nowadays."

Diane stared at her, creases appearing between her finely drawn brows. "She was a slut," she said, beginning to slur her words.

Clara caught her breath. Had Lisa been telling the truth about the affair? Had Diane found out and decided to get rid of her competition? She pretended to be shocked. "Excuse me?"

Diane took another gulp of her glass and set it down firmly enough to slop some of the liquid over the side. "Lisa Warren slept with anyone who asked her. There were even rumors that she was involved with my husband." She hiccupped, and placed a hand over her mouth. "Excuse me."

Clara chose her next words very carefully. "But of course, they were lies."

"Of course they were lies." Diane leaned back in her chair and closed her eyes. "I went to the office to confront her."

Afraid the woman would nod off, Clara asked quickly, "What happened?"

Diane opened her eyes again. "She wasn't there. So I searched her desk drawers to see if I could find anything incriminating."

She slurred the last word so badly Clara had to guess what she'd said. "But you didn't find anything."

Diane sat up so suddenly she made Clara jump. "Ah, but I did." She waved her hand in the air as if she were trying to fan herself, then reached for her glass again. "I found a note."

Clara watched her take another gulp of gin. "A note?"

Diane nodded, but said nothing.

After a long pause, Clara prompted, "What did it say?"

Diane leaned forward and lifted a shaking finger to her lips. "Shhh. Don't tell anyone."

Hoping she wouldn't notice the recorder on the table, Clara shook her head. "I won't."

Her hopes were dashed when Diane flapped her hand at the recorder. "Turn that thing off and I'll tell you."

Reluctantly, Clara switched it off.

Diane held out her hand. "Give it to me."

She handed it over and watched Diane fiddle with it until she was satisfied. "It was a note from Paul," she said at last, "telling Lisa to meet him behind the concert stage at eight p.m."

Clara stared at her. It was the last thing she'd expected. No wonder Diane wanted her to turn off the recorder. But why would the woman tell her about such damning evidence against her husband?

Once more Diane read her thoughts. "He didn't kill her." She shook her head slowly from side to side. "Nope, he didn't. You know how I know?"

Clara gave a quick shake of her head.

"I went there!" Diane beamed, as if she'd done something incredibly clever. "Yes, indeedy. I went behind that lil' ol' concert stage and I waited for 'em."

Clara couldn't have moved at that moment if the ceiling had caved in. She waited, barely able to breathe as Diane sat there nodding her head.

After another long, suspenseful pause, the woman raised a finger and shook it at Clara. "They didn't turn up."

Clara blinked. "They didn't?"

"Nope. I waited until ten past eight for them, and then I knew that note wasn't from Paul. My husband has never been late for anything in his life. If he said he was going to be there at eight p.m., he would have been there at ten minutes before eight. For eighteen years he's driven me crazy, always having to be somewhere at least ten minutes before he's due." She shook the finger again. "I keep telling him it doesn't matter if we're ten minutes late, but nope, he'll kill himself every time to get there early."

Clara frowned. "What about Lisa? You didn't see her?"

"Nope. Lisa was just the opposite. Always late to everything. Drove Paul nuts." Diane swallowed some more gin. "He was going to fire her, you know. He was just waiting to find the right person to take over for her."

"Did Lisa know that?"

Diane shrugged. "Dunno."

"Did you ask Paul about the note?"

Diane gazed at her bleary-eyed. "What?"

"The note. Did you ask Paul about it?"

Diane shook her head. "As soon as I heard about the murder, I flushed it down the toilet. I didn't want anyone suspecting my husband of killing Lisa." She leaned forward, her words running together, making them hard to understand. "He didn't write it. Someone else wrote that note to lure Lisa to the concert stage that night."

Clara was silent, trying to digest what she'd just heard.

Apparently realizing she'd said too much, Diane sounded worried when she spoke again. "Paul wasn't even there when Lisa died. He got a flat tire and stopped to have dinner on the way home. He didn't get back to the rodeo until it was almost over. Lisa was killed long before that."

"Then he has nothing to worry about." Clara held out her hand. "May I have my recorder back now?"

Diane clutched the little device to her chest. "You can't tell a soul about the note. It's gone and there's no proof it ever existed. I'll swear you're lying and it'll be your word against mine. I know—"

She closed her mouth as the door opened and Stephanie walked in, looking a little desperate as Mrs. Schwartz hovered behind her. "I have the photos," she said, signaling with her eyes her desire to leave immediately.

Apparently Diane had had enough as well. "Show them out," she said abruptly. She tossed the recorder at Clara, then leaned back and closed her eyes.

Clara stood, slipping the recorder into her purse before following her cousin out the door.

"She sounded drunk," Stephanie said when the house-keeper had firmly shut the front door behind them.

"She drank enough gin to put her on the floor." Clara led the way down the steps to the car. The sun had set behind the hills, leaving a humid night to take over. Crickets chirped in the grass, and moonlight bathed the driveway as she drove toward the gates. They opened just before she reached them and she passed through, realizing that security cameras must be tracking her movements. The thought made her uneasy, though she wasn't sure why.

"So what did she have to say?" Stephanie demanded, as they drove down the road leading to the highway.

"A lot." Clara recited as much as she could remember of her conversation with Diane Eastcott.

Stephanie kept punctuating her cousin's monologue with exclamations, finally breathing a soft "Whoa," when Clara told her about the note. "We have to tell Dan about that."

"She'll swear she didn't say any of it." Clara sighed. "She's right. Without the note to back it up, there's no proof."

"But you have it on the recorder."

"Nope. She made me turn it off." With one hand on the wheel, Clara fished the recorder out of her purse. "Here. This is all I got on there."

Stephanie took it from her, fiddled with it for a moment

or two, then muttered, "You don't have anything on here. It's blank."

Clara shot her a startled look. "Blank?"

"Not a peep on here."

"Diane must have erased the whole thing. Why would she do that?"

"Maybe she knew she sounded bombed and didn't want anyone else to hear it."

"But what about my interview?"

"We have the photos, if you really want to go ahead with it. Then again, she can't blame you for dumping the interview if she erased the whole thing."

"Well, I don't care what she says, or what her sleaze of a husband says, I think he was lying about having dinner at the Pioneer Inn." Clara glanced in her mirrors before turning onto the highway. "I think he killed Lisa, and somehow we have to find a way to prove it."

"I thought you were convinced Wes Carlton was the killer."

"I was, but after talking to Diane, I'm pretty sure it was Paul."

"You think he really did write that note?"

"Yes, I do. I think Diane knows it, too."

Stephanie sat back on her seat. "Well, I have something that might help."

With a glimmer of hope, Clara glanced at her cousin. "What is it?"

"There were two enormous walk-in closets in the master bedroom. I took pictures of them with my phone."

"Closets? Why would you take pics of them?"

"I took pics of what was *in* them. Paul has two red shirts hanging up there."

Clara gasped. "Really?"

"What was even more interesting"—Stephanie lowered her voice—"is that Diane has one, too." ·

11

"So we have to add Diane to our list of suspects." Touching the brake with her toe, Clara slowed down for the traffic light at the edge of town. "One of them is lying. The question is, which one?"

"How many suspects do we have now?" Stephanie held up her fingers one by one. "Wes Carlton, Paul Eastcott, Diane Eastcott—anyone else?"

"We haven't ruled out Anita Beaumont," Clara reminded her.

"Oh, yeah. Then there's always the possibility that someone else outside of the rodeo had it in for Lisa. She's not exactly Snow White."

"Maybe, but we're looking for motive, and all our

suspects had a motive to get rid of Lisa Warren. All those motives are tied to her relationship with Paul Eastcott, and since she was in love with him, it's unlikely she was involved with anyone else. Besides, in my vision I saw a cowboy in a red shirt standing over her, remember? How many cowboys do you see around Finn's Harbor?"

"True. So then, what about Diane? Maybe she dressed as a cowboy for the rodeo. Let's suppose Paul did write the note, then got delayed with that flat tire. Diane could have waited for Lisa to turn up behind the stage and, in a fit of jealousy, strangled her."

"Possible, but then it's unlikely she would have just happened to stumble across Wes's pigging string."

Stephanie sighed. "Okay, so what do you think happened?"

Slowing down again, Clara turned onto her cousin's street. "I think Paul wrote the note, intending to break it off with Lisa. He got the flat tire, which made him late getting to the meeting place. Diane had already left when he got there. Lisa was also late—Diane said she made a habit of it—and when Paul tried to dump her she threatened to tell his wife. So he had to silence her."

"But what about the pigging string?"

Clara frowned. "Maybe he intended all along to get rid of Lisa, and stole the pigging string to make it look like Wes killed her." She pulled up outside Stephanie's house. "I need time to think about this. My head is spinning with all this stuff. We'll talk about it tomorrow."

"Okay." Stephanie climbed out of the car, then stuck her head back in the door. "Hope you sleep well."

"You, too." Clara waited until her cousin had disappeared inside the house before pulling away from the curb. It seemed an eternity until she reached home, though it was only a few blocks away. Tatters was at the door when she put her key in the lock and opened it.

"I know, boy," Clara said wearily. "You need to go for a walk."

Tatters wagged his tail. *Yeah!*

"You'll have to wait until I talk to Mom." Walking into the room, Clara smiled at her mother, who sat, as usual, in front of the TV, her nightly glass of wine at her side. She looked anxious when she asked, "So how did your meeting with Diane Eastcott go?"

Clara sank onto the couch and stretched out her feet. "She's an interesting woman." Hoping to avoid any more questions, she quickly changed the subject. "By the way, I've invited Rick over for dinner on Tuesday."

Jessie sat up, her eyes sparkling with delight. "You did? That's wonderful! I'll have to come up with one of my specialties."

"Actually," Clara said carefully, "I was thinking of cooking the dinner myself." She looked down at Tatters, who was sniffing her knees.

"Oh." Looking deflated, her mother sank back on her chair. "Well, if you really want to do that . . ." Her voice trailed off with a sigh.

Clara gently pushed the dog away. "I would like to use one of your recipes, though."

Jessie brightened again at once. "Of course! We'll have such fun deciding which one. I'll get them now and we'll look through them."

She started to get up, and Clara said quickly, "Tomorrow. I have to take Tatters for a walk now."

At the word *walk*, Tatters' ears pricked up.

"Oh, okay." Her mother leaned back again. "So did you find out anything about the murder?"

Clara hoped her guilty start hadn't been too obvious. "What do you mean?"

"Isn't that why you went to see Diane Eastcott? You told me you were going to interview her for an article, but as far as I know, you've never been interested in writing." Jessie reached for her glass. "On the other hand, you've developed a strong and incredibly risky desire to take over Dan's job as police chief."

Clara had to laugh. "Don't tell Dan that."

Tatters pushed his nose into her hand, and she scratched his ear.

I smell cats.

Clara snatched her hand away.

Her mother gave her a shrewd look before taking a sip from her glass. "I just hope," she said, as she put the glass down again, "that you've learned your lesson from past mistakes. Murderers don't make the best playmates."

"Don't worry." Clara got up from the couch. "I have

no intention of getting that close to a murderer again. I'm just asking a few questions, that's all."

"I seem to have heard that before. Right before the cavalry had to come and rescue you." She leaned forward. "Promise me, Clara, you won't go chasing after criminals again. I've lost one love of my life. I couldn't bear to lose you, too."

Clara patted her shoulder. "Don't worry, Mom. I'll be careful." With a quick wave of her hand, she left the room, with Tatters following close on her heels.

Once outside in the street, she looked down at the dog, who sat staring at her with an accusing look in his eyes. "All right," she said softly, "we have a cat in the store now. Since I have no intention of taking you there, you don't need to worry about it."

Tatters didn't even twitch.

"He's Molly's cat, not mine."

Still the dog remained motionless.

Clara sighed. "I still love you best. I always will."

With that, Tatters stood, shook himself and stalked off down the street.

Hanging on to the leash, Clara hurried to catch up to him. Her mother's parting shot had made her uneasy, and she tried to put it out of her mind as she followed the dog down the street to the beach. Maybe her mother was right. Maybe she should tell Dan what she'd learned from Diane, and let him take care of it from there.

She'd come close to losing her life before when she'd

asked the wrong people too many questions. Maybe it was time to butt out.

Her moment of truth came the following afternoon, when Tim strolled into the bookstore and stopped at the counter to ask her which books she would recommend for his uncle's birthday.

Clara checked through the list of their latest orders, her mind wrestling with the question of whether or not she should tell Tim what she knew. On the one hand, it could help in the investigation. On the other hand, since there was only Diane's word to go on, she could be getting herself into trouble for no reason.

"Any more news on the murder investigation?" she asked lightly, after she'd given Tim some titles to check out.

Tim gave her a wary look. "Not yet." He jammed his hands in his pockets. "The rodeo packs up and leaves tomorrow. Looks like this will go down as a cold case."

Clara wrestled with her conscience a moment or two longer, than blurted out, "I might have something that could help."

Tim narrowed his eyes. "So tell me."

As briefly as possible, she repeated the story Diane had given her. "I know you can't prove anything without the note," she said, when she was done, "but it does point you to a strong suspect in the case."

To her dismay, Tim shook his head. "We've already cleared Paul Eastcott. He was having dinner at the Pioneer

Inn during the time Lisa was killed. He has a receipt to prove it."

A receipt. Why hadn't they thought of that? "So that lets Paul off the hook. What about Diane? She admitted to being behind the concert stage just before Lisa was killed."

Tim smiled. "Do you really think she'd admit that if she'd killed Lisa?"

Clara wouldn't have put anything past Diane, but she thought it best not to say so.

"In any case," Tim added, "we're pretty sure Carlton is our guy. We just can't prove it. Yet. He's been ordered not to leave town, and we're keeping an eye on him, hoping something breaks. And that's probably more than I should have told you, so I'm going to take a look at these books now. By the way, you'd better not let Dan find out you're asking questions again." With that, he wandered off down one of the aisles.

Clara stared at the list of orders on the computer screen. So it was back to Wes. Much as she hated to admit it, now that Paul was off the list, Wes seemed the likely candidate for the crime. Tim was right. No matter how drunk she was, Diane was too smart to admit she was at the crime scene if she'd killed Lisa. In any case, somehow she just couldn't see Diane as a cold-blooded murderer.

It didn't seem as if there was anything else she could do. She hated the thought of Wes getting away with murder. On the other hand, she hated the thought of Rick finding out his longtime buddy was a killer even more.

She needed to talk to Stephanie. Even while the thought was forming, she was calling her cousin's number.

Stephanie answered right away. "What's up?"

Clara told her everything Tim had said. "It looks like it could be Wes after all," she said, as Stephanie groaned.

"So what are we going to do now?"

"Nothing." Clara glanced at the clock. "What can we do? The rodeo's last show begins in an hour or so, then they'll pack up and move on. Everyone except Wes, that is. Dan told him he can't leave town."

"How long can they keep him here under suspicion?"

"I don't know. Long enough to ruin his career, I should think. If he is the killer, it's the least he deserves."

"What if he isn't the killer? What if Dan doesn't solve the case? Someone is going to get away with murder."

"I know." Clara gazed miserably out the window. "I hate it as much as you do." Her eye fell on the poster plastered to the window. "How's Molly doing? Is she going to the rodeo tonight?"

"Yes, she is. Since it was her day off today, she had plenty of time to rest. She called me a little while ago and said she felt well enough to go. She really doesn't want to miss it."

"Well, great. I'm glad someone is having a good day. I'll call you later." She hung up and turned back to the computer. The new orders were due to go out, and since

Molly had been sick, nothing had been done about contacting any authors about book signings.

After sending out the orders, Clara sent off e-mails to the list of authors Stephanie had given her who might be interested in doing a signing.

The evening dragged by after that, with few customers to relieve the monotony. She passed the time by reading the back blurbs of popular authors' books, in the hopes that she could answer any questions that might come up. Some customers acted as if they expected her to have read every single book in the store.

Feeling immeasurably tired, she locked up shortly after eight and stepped out onto the street. The lights were already out in Rick's store, which meant he'd gone home. She felt a fierce urge to see him as she walked down the hill to the parking lot. It took her by surprise, and she shrugged it off. She'd see him tomorrow night. For dinner. At her house.

As usual, every time she thought about that her stomach turned over. She didn't know if she was worried more about Jessie asking too many personal questions or about having to make dinner for a gourmet cook.

Tomorrow would be her day off, so she had all day to worry about it. Jessie had fished out a few recipes and together they'd settled on a walnut pear salad, honey-glazed salmon with roasted potatoes and brandied peaches for dessert. Simple dishes with a dynamite taste.

Thinking about food made her stomach rumble, and

she wasted no time in getting home. Tatters greeted her at the door, as usual, and a familiar heavenly aroma drifted from the kitchen. Oregano, Clara decided, as she crossed the empty living room to the kitchen. Definitely a touch of garlic. Her mother was making chicken Marsala.

Her mother stood at the stove, a wooden spoon in her hand and a pot simmering in front of her. She looked over her shoulder as Clara walked in. "Ah, there you are. I figured since you were cooking dinner tomorrow, I'd make my specialty tonight. I know it's your favorite."

"It is, and I'm starving." Clara walked over to the fridge and opened it. "Chardonnay or pinot?"

"Chardonnay." Jessie opened the oven and took out the warmed plates. "So how did your day go?"

"Okay. How was yours?" Clara uncorked the bottle of chardonnay and poured wine into two glasses.

Jessie glanced at her. "What's wrong?"

Clara smiled. "Who says anything is wrong?"

"Your voice does." Jessie frowned. "Are you having second thoughts about asking Rick over for dinner?"

"No, of course not." She'd said it just a little too quickly, and she hurried to add, "It will be fun. I have all day to get ready for it, so there's no pressure."

"Except your boyfriend is getting to meet your mother for the first time," Jessie said dryly. She started serving the chicken onto the plates.

Clara carried the wine over to the kitchen table and sat down. "Rick told me you'd already met."

Jessie avoided her gaze. "Hmm, well, I did go into his store a few days ago. I needed some wall hangers for a painting."

"What painting?"

"I haven't exactly bought it yet." She placed the plates on the table. "But I'm going to, soon."

Clara picked up her fork. "You went in there just to check him out."

Jessie sat down opposite her. "Okay, so I was curious." She lifted her glass and sipped the wine. "He's a very nice young man."

"Yes, he is."

They were both silent for a moment or two while they tasted the chicken. Then Jessie said abruptly, "You're worried I'll ask him too many personal questions."

Clara put down her fork. "You do have a tendency to interrogate people."

"Interrogate?" Jessie looked hurt. "I'm just interested in people, that's all. I don't mean to pry into their private lives. If they don't want to talk about it, that's fine."

Clara sighed. "Look, I'll fill you in on what I know. That way, you won't have to ask. Then if Rick adds anything of his own accord, it will be new to both of us."

"All right." Jessie dug into her chicken again. "So why isn't he married? He's good-looking, successful and very well-mannered. A man like that should have a wife and kids."

"He was married. He has no kids. His wife didn't want them. He did. He's now divorced."

"Oh." Jessie digested the news while chomping on her chicken. "Well, I can see how that might cause problems in a marriage. Where is she now? His wife, I mean?"

"I don't know. I didn't ask."

"Have you met her?"

"No, and I have no desire to do so."

"Not even a picture of her?"

"Not even a picture." Clara took a gulp of her wine. "You'll probably be happy to know that I've given up asking questions about Lisa Warren's murder."

Jessie's face lit up with relief. "You have? Oh, I'm so happy to hear that. What made you give up?"

Having steered her mother away from the subject of Rick, Clara phrased her answer with care. "Well, the person I thought was guilty actually has a solid alibi, and since I have no clue who else might be guilty, I figured it was time I let Dan take care of it."

Jessie looked intrigued. "I figured you were doing more than just asking questions. So who did you think was the killer?"

Clara shrugged. "I thought it might be Paul Eastcott, but I was wrong."

"Well, I have to tell you, I couldn't be more pleased. I never did know why you felt so compelled to get involved in such a nasty business. It's dangerous enough for the police, and much more so for someone like you, who has no experience or training. I think . . ."

Clara sat very still. Her mother's voice had faded away, and the kitchen walls dissolved into a gray mist. The arena appeared before her. She could feel the hard bench beneath her, and a stiff breeze ruffling her hair. The sun shone full in her eyes, making it hard to see the two figures in the middle of the arena.

She shaded her eyes with her hand, and now she could see that the figures were clowns. One was Marty, in the familiar black and white checkered coat and striped pants. The other clown, in a bright blue suit and red wig, looked familiar, too.

As she watched, a movement caught her eye. Standing in front of the chutes stood a huge bull, pawing at the ground. She cried out, but as usual, could make no sound. The clowns must have heard the bull, however, as they both turned and raced toward him.

Holding her breath, Clara watched as the bull lowered his head and charged. Marty danced around him, and the bull thundered past, missing him by inches with his lethal horns. Then the other clown leapt forward, waving his arms. The bull charged again, and the clown dodged sideways. He wasn't quite quick enough. The bull caught him with one of his horns and tossed the clown in the air.

Shuddering, Clara shut her eyes. When she opened

them again she was no longer in the arena. It was night-time now, and only a dim glow from a streetlamp pene-trated the shadows in the parking lot. The breeze had cooled, chilling her bare arms.

She heard the roar of an engine and the pickup burst into view, heading straight at her. Every instinct urged her to jump out of the way, but she could see a shadowy figure at the wheel, and she desperately wanted to see the face of the driver.

The truck drew closer and closer, and still she stood her ground. Only a few more seconds and she could see—

"You're having a vision, aren't you?"

Clara jumped and opened her eyes.

She was back in the kitchen, and her mother sat across from her, studying her with an intent look on her face.

Clara drew a deep breath. "I'm what?"

"You're having a vision. I've seen that look a dozen times or more on your father's face, and now I'm seeing it on yours. You have the Quinn Sense."

"That's crazy. I don't—"

"Yes, you do. I'm your mother. I know."

Clara slumped her shoulders. "How long have you known?"

"For a while. Since you came back from New York." Jessie sipped her wine and set down the glass. "Why didn't you tell me?"

"I didn't want anyone to know. I still don't."

Jessie's brow cleared. "You especially don't want Rick to know."

"Right."

Jessie stared at her glass for a moment, then said quietly, "I know you care a great deal for this young man. I'm assuming he feels the same way. How long do you think you can keep something like this from him?"

"For as long as I possibly can."

"Is that fair to him? What if you have one of these visions while you're with him? How are you going to explain it?"

"I already have. He thinks I have a problem with indigestion." Clara leaned forward and fixed a hard stare on her mother's face. "I absolutely forbid you to tell anyone else about this. Especially Rick."

Jessie shook her head. "Of course I won't say anything. That's your obligation, not mine."

"Obligation?"

"Would you want him to keep something like that from you?"

"Maybe not, but I'd understand."

"Well, let's hope he does too, when he finds out." Jessie pushed her chair back. "I'll do the dishes. You go ahead and make your call to Stephanie. She's probably waiting to hear that she's still in business. That woman worries far too much about everything."

Clara had to smile at that, since Jessie was a chronic

worrywart. Her smile soon faded, however, as she walked into her bedroom, Tatters anxiously hovering at her heels. Maybe her mother was right. Maybe Rick did have a right to know about her weird inheritance.

She should talk to him. Try to explain about the Quinn Sense, and what it was. Sitting down at the computer, she buried her head in her hands. He was never going to understand. He'd think she was completely off her rocker and do his best to avoid her after that. She couldn't talk to him about it. There was just no way.

Trying to shake the anxiety that threatened to overwhelm her, she turned on her computer. After zapping a dozen or so spam e-mails, she saw one with a file attached. It had been sent to both her and Stephanie from Molly.

The file turned out to be pictures from the rodeo that Molly had sent from her phone, with the message, "Having a blast at the rodeo!"

The first pic was of a barrel racer, caught going at full speed across the arena. The girl's hat had slipped from her head and hung on her back, while her long red hair streamed behind her. She leaned across her horse's neck, her face a mask of grim determination.

Recognizing Anita Beaumont, Clara studied the photo a moment or two longer before clicking on the next one. This one was of Sparky the clown, capturing the moment he burst a balloon over his head.

Molly had quite an eye for photography, Clara thought, as she clicked through the next five pics. Any one of them would be good enough to win a contest. She'd be sure to mention it to the young assistant when she saw her on Wednesday.

The last pic was of the finale. Clara glanced at the clock. A little after ten. Molly must have sent the pics moments ago, as the rodeo had only just ended. She looked back at the last photo. The presentation was spectacular, with all the contestants, most of them on horseback, circling the arena. The clowns bounced around in the center, while Sparky had let go a bunch of balloons, allowing them to float up into the air.

She clicked through the pics again, aware of an odd sense that something wasn't quite right. She took another long look at Anita's photo, then paused at the one of Sparky bursting the balloon. He seemed different somehow, though she couldn't think why. She saved the pic to a file and enlarged it. Marty Pearce's face stared back at her, his yellow lips curved into a massive grin.

Everything about him looked the same, and yet she couldn't rid herself of the niggling feeling that something was off.

Switching to a search engine, she brought up the local news station. There was a video of the opening night of the rodeo—just a few clips from the performance. She found the one of Marty and ran it. The clown went through his routine, just as she remembered seeing it.

But there it was again, that weird feeling that something wasn't right.

Wes had thought the same thing that night. He'd said that Marty was off his game. She ran the video again, but still couldn't see anything weird or different about the clown.

A soft sound behind her turned her head. Tatters sat there staring at her with soulful eyes.

Are you going to sit there all night, or are we going for a walk?

"Okay, Tats." She got up from the computer. "Let's go. I could use some fresh air. I'll call Steffie when we get back."

Grabbing her jacket on the way out, she called out to Jessie that she was taking the dog for a walk and stepped outside. The night breezes from the sea cooled the air enough for her to pull on her jacket as she followed Tatters at a brisk pace toward the beach.

There were few people about now that darkness had settled in, and she reached the beach without passing anyone. Tatters strained at his leash, anxious to be free to dash onto the sand. Mindful of the time she'd lost sight of him in the dark, Clara tugged him back.

"You stay close enough for me to see you, understand?" She wagged a finger at him. "If you don't, it will be the last time I let you off the leash."

The light from the streetlamp lit up the dog's eyes, flashing gold in his black, furry face.

Spoilsport.

She sighed. "I don't want to lose you, Tats. Be reasonable." She glanced over her shoulder, worried someone might hear her asking a dog to be reasonable, for heaven's sake. That reminded her of the moment she'd found out her mother knew about the Sense.

Jessie was right, she thought, as she followed Tatters down the steps and watched him leaping toward the water. If she was going to have any hope of a real relationship with Rick, she needed to tell him everything.

She came to a halt, shocked that she was actually hoping for a serious relationship. After being practically dumped at the altar in New York, she'd sworn never to get that involved again. Yet here she was, scared to death Rick would walk away once he found out what a weirdo he was dating.

It shook her to realize just how much she would hate that.

Deep in thought, she wandered down to the water's edge, where Tatters was wrestling with a large piece of seaweed. "You'll choke on that," she said, then pulled a face when she realized how much she sounded like her mother.

Tatters ignored her, and played happily in and out of the water until his coat was soaked and covered in sand. He was reluctant to leave his ideal playground, and she had to call him twice, threatening to ground him if he didn't obey.

He finally left the water and plodded up the sand toward the steps, his tail swinging back and forth behind him.

One more mess for her to clean up, Clara thought, as she

trudged after him. Reaching the top of the steps, she fastened his leash to his collar. "Okay, boy. Time to go home."

Remembering that Rick was coming to dinner tomorrow night, she started worrying all over again. Deep in thought, she stepped off the curb to cross the street with Tatters at her side.

She was halfway across the road when she heard the engine and saw the lights glowing out of the darkness. She froze, mindless of Tatters straining to pull her to safety. The truck was heading straight for her, and she seemed unable to move. Was she having a vision? It didn't seem like it, yet she couldn't seem to get up enough energy to move.

She let go of the leash, and Tatters barked a warning. *Run!*

Her feet seemed glued to the ground. She shut her eyes against the glare of the headlights, and waited.

In the next instant she felt a hard thump between her shoulder blades, which sent her flying to the edge of the road. Ending up sprawled onto the hard ground, she felt the thunder of tires and the rush of wind as the truck grazed past her. She was alive. *Thank God.*

One thing she did know—this was no vision. The sting of her scraped elbows and knees was testimony to that.

She turned her head, panic draining every ounce of energy she had left. *Tatters.* He was gone. She called his name, her voice sounding weak and high-pitched. Ears straining, she squinted in the dark, half afraid to see his still body lying in the road.

She could see nothing. Again she called his name, and this time heard a faint whimper in the distance. *Oh, please, no!* He'd been hit. She scrambled to her feet, prayers tumbling from her lips. The dog had saved her. Please, God, don't let him have sacrificed his own life for hers.

12

Starting across the street, Clara was aware of screeching brakes. Farther down the road, the truck was backing up toward her.

She ignored it, intent on finding out what had happened to Tatters. He must have leapt at her to shove her out of the way. If he'd been hit she'd kill that driver. She frantically called his name. "Tatters? *Tatters!* Where are you?"

Another feeble whine answered her from across the street.

The truck was almost on her now, and she tore across the road toward the sound she'd heard. She could just see the dog's head above the deep ditch running alongside the road. "Tatters!"

She fell on her knees beside him, heedless of the uneven footsteps coming toward her. Tears spilled on her cheeks and she dashed them away. "Are you hurt? Don't move. I'll get help."

She jumped as a deep voice spoke behind her. "Are you okay? I didn't see you in the dark. Did I hit you? I didn't feel anything, but—"

She looked up into Marty's anxious face. He looked pale in the glow from the streetlamp, and for a brief moment she felt sorry for him. Then anger took over. "I think you hit my dog."

"What? Oh God. I'm so sorry." He moved closer, and Tatters growled.

Turning back to the dog, Clara patted his head and said tearfully, "Don't move, boy. We'll get help."

Quit that. I'm fine.

She stared at him. "What?"

I'm stuck. Get me out of here.

Mindful of Marty leaning over her, Clara swallowed her relief. "I don't think he's hurt after all," she said, gripping Tatters' collar. "He must have jumped in there. Can you help me lift him out?"

"Sure." Grunting, Marty got down on his knees, and together they hauled Tatters out of the narrow ditch.

Throwing her arms around the dog's neck, Clara whispered, "Are you sure you're not hurt?"

For answer, Tatters licked her face.

Even so, she walked him back and forth a few times

just to reassure herself. He limped a bit but otherwise seemed okay. When she was satisfied, she faced Marty. "You could have killed us both."

"I know." Marty ran a hand through his hair. "I'm so sorry. I was looking for you. I remember you saying you took the dog for a walk around this time. I didn't know where you lived so I came looking for you here. I just didn't see you in the dark until I was almost on top of you."

Still shaken, Clara let out her breath. "Well, okay. Luckily there's no harm done. Why were you looking for me, anyway?"

"Actually, Wes sent me. There's something he wants to tell you."

Clara frowned. "Why didn't he come himself?"

"He can't. The cops are watching his every move. He said it's important he talks to you alone."

"Why didn't he call me?"

"He doesn't have your number." Marty lowered his voice, as if afraid of being overheard. "He said to tell you he found out something about Lisa's murder that you should know."

"Did he tell you what it was?"

"No, he wouldn't say."

Tatters stirred at her side and she didn't need the Sense to tell her what he was thinking. "Why doesn't he tell the police if he has new evidence?"

Marty opened the passenger door of his truck. "I asked him that. He said he needs to talk to you first. He's afraid the police won't believe him. Hop in and I'll take you there."

"Take me where?"

"He's waiting for us in the arena."

She stared at him for a long moment. Could she really trust this man? Why would Wes send him instead of Rick? What if Marty was Lisa's killer, trying to lure her somewhere in order to silence her? In the next instant she dismissed the thought. This was Sparky the clown. The man who loved children and lived to entertain them. The man who himself was in danger from the killer. The Sense had convinced her of that much. Wes could have tried to get ahold of Rick and failed.

Marty half closed the truck door. "Look, I understand if you don't want to go. I don't blame you. It's just that Wes sounded so upbeat about this. I really believe he's found out who the true killer is and is excited about getting his name cleared."

Still she hesitated. Her instincts told her she'd be crazy to meet a suspected murderer in an empty arena after dark. What if Wes was worried she would find evidence that he killed Lisa and had decided to get rid of her, too? Then again, it wasn't that late. Surely other people would still be wandering around, perhaps doing cleanup chores.

She had to be nuts. What had happened to her decision to let Dan handle things from now on? On the other hand, if Wes wanted to kill her, would he send another person to bring her into a trap? Unless he planned to kill Marty, too.

None of it made sense. The only way she was going to find out what was going on was to go talk to Wes. "I'll go if you'll stay with me while I talk to him," she said at last.

"Of course I will." Marty patted her shoulder. "Don't worry, honey. I'm convinced Wes didn't kill Lisa. He just wants to talk to you, that's all."

If that were true, she so badly wanted to know what it was Wes had found out. If Wes wasn't the murderer, he could know something that would lead Dan to Lisa's killer. He knew she was trying to help him. Maybe he really was innocent, and trusted her more than he trusted the police.

"All right." She looked down at Tatters. "I'll have to bring the dog along."

"That's okay." Marty gave her a little bow, his arm outstretched. "Hop in."

Clara noticed the dog stumbled a bit when he jumped up the step into the cab. She helped him up on the seat, whispering urgently to him while Marty walked around the front of the truck to the driver's side. "You did get hurt, didn't you?"

Tatters held up a paw and flinched when she touched it.

She waited for Marty to climb up and start the engine. "I think I'm going to drop Tatters off at home first, if that's okay? It's not far out of our way. He's limping a bit and he needs to rest."

Hey! No way!

"You're going home," Clara said firmly.

Marty gave her a strange look and she hastily told him how to get to her house. Moments later he pulled up outside.

"I won't be more than a minute or two," she told him, then jumped down from the cab. Tatters followed her, stumbling once more as his right front paw hit the pavement.

His brief yelp of pain convinced her, and even Tatters offered no resistance as she led him into her bedroom.

He jumped up on the bed and looked at her.

"You worry too much. You're as bad as Jessie." Clara took her cell phone from her pocket. "If it will make you feel better, I'll try to call Rick. I'm sure he'd want to know I'm meeting Wes. I'll ask him to meet us at the arena."

Tatters slumped down and rested his jaw on his paws.

Clara dialed Rick's number and waited. After a couple of buzzes his voice mail answered. That helped reassure her. Wes must have gotten Rick's voice mail too, and, eager to report his discovery as soon as possible, had asked Marty, instead, to find her.

Quickly she thumbed out a text message and sent it to Rick. She gave a brief thought to calling Stephanie, then decided against it. Her cousin would want to know all the details, and Marty was waiting outside. "Rick should get my message," she said, as she slipped the phone back into her pocket. "Now stay here until I get back, okay? First thing tomorrow we go see the vet."

Tatters raised his head. *I don't need a vet. I'm fine*. He flapped a paw at her for emphasis.

"I hope so." She leaned forward and wrapped her arms about his neck. "You saved my life tonight, Tats. I won't forget that. Thank you."

He made a grumbling sound deep in his throat, and after a quick kiss on his nose, she let him go. "I'll be back as soon as I can."

Jessie had already gone to bed, though she called out as Clara passed by her door. "Is everything okay?"

Clara hesitated, then answered carefully, "Sure. I'm just dropping Tatters off. I have to go out for a bit."

"Where are you going this time of night?"

"I won't be long!" Clara headed for the front door and slipped through it, closing it quietly behind her. There'd be time for an interrogation when she got back. For now, all her attention was on the meeting with Wes.

As she climbed back into Marty's truck, she had to admit to a certain amount of anxiety. She tried to calm her fears, reminding herself that Marty would be there, and if Rick got her message in time, he'd be there, too. Settling back on her seat, she tried to relax. It was too late now to change her mind. She was on her way to talk to Wes Carlton and, with any luck, solve a murder.

———

"It's really strange," Stephanie said, plopping herself down on the couch next to George.

"Everything is really strange around here." George pointed the remote at the blaring TV and shut off the sound. "What in particular is strange tonight?"

"Clara hasn't called." Stephanie glanced at the clock on the crowded mantelpiece. It was a little hard to see since the face was almost covered by the shield of a knight in armor that had somehow been knocked sideways. "She usually calls right after dinner."

"She's probably taking that hound for a walk. Or, I should say, letting him take her for a walk. That dog is bigger than my car."

Stephanie rolled her eyes. "You do love to exaggerate." She got up and walked over to the computer desk. "I'll call her and see what's up. I hope she's not sick or something." She unplugged the phone from the charger and carried it back to the couch, dialing Clara's speed dial number on the way.

Clara's voice mail answered her and she left a message. "That's odd. She always answers when she knows it's me calling her."

George turned the TV sound back on. "She's probably out on a date with Rick."

"She would have told me if she had a date with him."

"Maybe she didn't know. It could have been a last-minute thing."

"Still, you'd think she'd answer her phone." Stephanie thrust the phone into her pants pocket. "For all she knows, I could have an emergency or something."

"You're always having an emergency or something." George put his arm around his wife and pulled her close. "Relax. If Clara was in trouble, you'd be the first one she'd call."

"Yeah, I guess you're right." Stephanie did her best to put her worry out of her mind. "She might have taken Tatters for a walk and forgot her phone. She'll call when she gets back." She settled down to watch the show, uncomfortably aware of the gnawing anxiety that wouldn't go away.

———

Clara hunched her shoulders as Marty drove into the fairgrounds. It was the first time she'd seen it without all the lights blaring and crowds milling about. The entire place was deserted. The only lights still on were the streetlamps, and their glow barely reached the walls of the arena.

Marty parked the truck in the empty parking lot and switched off the engine. The silence that surrounded them made the murky shadows seem all the more ominous.

Clara stared at the dark void of the arena, her shaky confidence draining away. "Can't you go and ask Wes to meet us out here?"

"He was firm about wanting to meet you in the arena." Marty opened his door. "I guess with the cops watching him all the time, he needed a place where he could slip away in private."

Wishing fervently she had Tatters with her, Clara climbed down from the cab. She was tempted to call Rick again, but Marty was already limping off into the dark, and she hurried after him, reluctant to be alone in the creepy shadows of the deserted fairgrounds.

She caught up with him, and together they entered the arena. The seats were all in darkness, and although Clara knew there was no one there, she felt as if unseen eyes stared at her from the stands.

Marty led her to the chutes, and halted in front of the gates. "This is where Wes said to wait for him." He raised his wrist to look at his watch, but apparently it was too dark for him to see it, as he dropped his arm with a shake of his head. "I'm sure he won't be long."

Clara could feel little tingles of apprehension tickling her neck. She moved over to one of the gates and pressed her back against the hard slats. It made her feel a little less vulnerable. Now that her eyes were getting adjusted to the dark, she could see the outline of the arena walls against the sky.

"So how long have you lived in Finn's Harbor?" Marty asked, leaning an elbow on top of the gate. A faint glow from a streetlamp fell across his chest, brightening the yellow shirt he wore.

Clara remembered the pic Molly had sent her. Marty had been wearing that shirt under his black and white suit that evening for the show. She'd noticed the bright splash of color at his chest. He must have kept it on when he changed into the jeans and jacket he wore now.

Aware that he was waiting for her answer, she made an effort to concentrate. "I was born here. I spent ten years in New York, but came back last year."

"Ah." Marty nodded his head. "You had to come back to your roots. I know how that feels."

Something was trying to surface in her mind. Something important. Was it about Wes? Something she should know? She tried to bring it into focus, but it slipped away again. Once more she had to force herself to make conversation. "So where were you born?"

Marty pushed himself away from the gate. "Me? I was born out west. Mesa, Arizona. It's a suburb of Phoenix."

"How long have you been with the rodeo?"

"Since I was old enough to sit on a horse. My daddy was a rodeo champ, and I wanted desperately to be just like him. He didn't fight the bulls—he rode 'em."

Clara tried to imagine Marty astride an irate, twisting, writhing bull and failed. "So what made you decide to be a clown?"

Marty made a harsh sound of disgust. "It was the only thing I was good enough at to survive the circuit. It's a tough world, and the competition is fierce. I soon gave up trying to keep up with the riders. I took too many falls. I knew I'd end up maimed or worse if I didn't let it go. So I took to bullfighting, and you know the rest."

"But you're a great clown. It must be so rewarding to know you can make people laugh like that."

He didn't answer at first, and when he did, his voice was thick with emotion. "I'd give it all up to be a wrangler like Wes. Clowns get no respect out there. People think that because I'm a clown they can laugh at anything and everything I say or do. They don't think I have feelings just like everybody else."

He sounded so miserable Clara felt an urge to hug him. "Oh, I'm sure they do. They just—"

"Hey, look at me, getting all sentimental." Marty chuckled, though it sounded forced. "I can't think what's keeping Wes. I'd better go and look for him. You should wait here 'til I get back, in case I miss him in the dark."

"Oh, I don't think . . . Wait! I don't . . ." She broke off as Marty scuttled off into the shadows, leaving her alone.

Her uneasiness plummeted into full-blown panic. *Where was Rick?* Had he seen her message? She pulled the phone from her pocket and held it up to see her contacts list. All she could see was a blank screen.

Frantically, she swiped the screen again and again. The phone was dead. Out of battery power. She cursed her forgetfulness. She'd meant to recharge it last night, but after her interview with Diane she'd gone to bed later than usual, and charging her cell had been the last thing on her mind.

She leaned her back against the gate again, trying to control the rapid beating of her heart. There was nothing to worry about. Marty would come back with Wes. He'd tell her what it was he'd found out, and then she could go to Dan and tell him and everything would turn out all right. Wes's name would be cleared, Rick would be happy for his friend and they could all celebrate.

She was picturing the celebration, perhaps at the fancy restaurant in the Hill Top Resort, when she thought she heard a sound. She straightened, one hand gripping the top slat of the gate. "Hello? Is anyone there?" She stared into the shifting shadows, trying to distinguish a movement. "Marty?" Then, even more hopefully, "Rick?"

No one answered her. She leaned back, and in the next instant, bright light dazzled her. She blinked, her mind grappling with this sudden change. It was daylight, the sun full in her eyes. She was back outside the Raven's Nest, staring at the window.

No, not the window. The poster in the window. Sparky the clown grinned back at her. What was the Sense trying to tell her? She stared at the poster, trying to understand the significance. And then it hit her. The black and white suit. The flash of red. Marty Pearce was wearing a red shirt under his suit.

The window melted away and grew dark, and she was back in the arena, the hard slats of the gate at her back. Heart thumping, she closed her eyes, visualizing the video she'd seen of the first night's performance. She was positive he wasn't wearing a yellow shirt that night. She would have noticed it on the video. Which meant he could have been wearing the red shirt.

She frowned, remembering something else about the video—Marty racing around the ring, turning cartwheels, tumbling over a giant ball.

She closed her eyes, visualizing the performance. Yes, she was certain. That night, Sparky the clown *had no limp*. She hadn't noticed Marty had a limp until she'd met him in the field the day after the performance.

Her mind working furiously, Clara started pacing back and forth. Had someone else played the clown that night? Was that why Wes had said the clown was off his game?

Something clicked into place. Seth Ferguson had once been a rodeo clown. What was it Grace had said? She thought back to the morning she had spent in Grace's living room, hearing again the widow's faltering words. *He smelled of the rodeo. Like he did when I first met him.*

At the time Clara had thought Seth had smelled of horses and sawdust. There was another possibility, however. The smell of greasepaint. She'd smelled it herself when she was talking to Marty the night she'd toured the rodeo backstage with Rick.

She paused, hearing again a sound from the other side of the arena. "Marty?" Her voice echoed around the empty stands, followed by an eerie silence.

More of Grace's words jumped into Clara's mind. The widow had found a wad of money in Seth's pocket. Had he been paid to play the clown?

Nerves jumping now, Clara began walking alongside the railings toward the exit of the arena. It all fit. Only one person would have paid Seth to take Marty's place that night.

It was Marty who had killed Lisa. He'd needed an alibi, and what better than thousands of noisy rodeo fans watching him? He'd hired Seth and given him a bundle of cash to play the clown that night.

Seth must have heard about Lisa's death and gotten suspicious. Maybe that's why he'd gone to the pub. Perhaps he'd had too much to drink and had confronted Marty. It had to be Marty who had killed Lisa. Marty who had run down Seth in the parking lot.

She shivered, hearing again the screech of brakes. A cold flash of fear shook her as she realized something else—the truck heading toward her on the coast road earlier that night. There had been no screech of brakes until long after the truck had passed. Marty had intended to run her down. *He was going to kill her.*

She started racing across the arena to the exit. She had no car, no phone. Her only hope was to outrun the crippled clown. She prayed he didn't have a gun, though she wouldn't be an easy target in the dark. She had almost reached the exit when she heard a sound that zapped all the strength from her legs.

The ominous thudding of hooves.

She didn't need lights to know what it meant. Stumbling, she looked over her shoulder. Sheer terror gripped her when she saw the shadowy outline of the bull, hooves pounding on the ground, charging straight at her.

Wes's words came back to her, clear and horrifying. *We've got one of his offspring. Ferocious. Just as mean. Make sure you keep out of his way.*

There was no doubt in her mind that this was Ferocious, the descendant of Bodacious, the world's most dangerous bull. And it was coming for her.

13

"I'm going to call Rick," Stephanie announced, as George turned off the TV. "Clara hasn't answered, and I'm worried about her."

"Do whatever it takes to help you quit worrying." George stretched his arms over his head and yawned. "But don't be surprised if your cousin yells at you for interrupting something intensely personal."

Stephanie raised her eyebrows. "Like what?"

George grinned. "Has it really been that long since we dated?"

"Oh!" Stephanie stared at her phone. "No. If Clara had gone on a date with Rick, she would have called me first. Something's wrong. I just know it."

George uttered a sigh of resignation. "So call him. You have his number?"

"Clara asked me to call him once. I added him to my contacts." She was dialing as she spoke. Rick's deep voice answered her and she spoke quickly, stumbling over the words in her anxiety. "Rick, it's Stephanie. Is Clara with you? If so, I'm so sorry to disturb you, but she didn't call me tonight and she always does and I'm just worried something might have happened to her and—"

"Whoa, whoa, slow down a minute." Rick sounded amused. "Clara's not here. She's probably out with Tatters."

"That's what I thought at first." Stephanie met her husband's questioning gaze and shook her head. "But I've been calling all evening and she's not answering her phone. She calls me every night when she gets home from the store. She never misses. She hasn't called tonight, and I just know something's wrong."

"I'm sure she's okay. What about her mom? Have you called her?"

"No, I didn't want to worry her. I guess I'll just wait to hear from Clara. Thanks, Rick. Sorry I disturbed you."

"Hey, no problem." He sounded concerned now, deepening Stephanie's anxiety. "Let me know when you hear from her, okay?"

"Sure." Stephanie hung up and sank onto the couch. "He hasn't heard from her. I hate to call Aunt Jessie. She could be in bed by now. If Clara's okay, I'll be waking up Aunt Jessie and getting her all worried over nothing."

George pulled her close. "You're probably worrying over nothing too, but I know you. You won't go to sleep until you know your cousin is safe and well. So go ahead and call your aunt."

"Yeah, you're right." Reluctantly she picked up the phone. As she did so, it jingled its call tone. Snatching it to her ear she asked breathlessly, "Clara?"

Her spirits sank when Rick's voice answered. "No, it's me. I thought I'd better let you know. Clara sent me a text. She must have called earlier while I was in the garage. I was using a buzz saw and didn't hear the phone."

"So what did the message say?"

"She said she was meeting Wes Carlton in the fairgrounds arena and wanted me to join them."

Stephanie uttered a little squeak. "She's meeting a murderer in the fairgrounds in the middle of the night?"

"Calm down. Wes didn't kill that woman. I'm sure of it." His voice tightened. "Though why Clara would want to meet Wes in an empty fairgrounds at night is something I don't understand. I'm going to call him. Hold on, and I'll get back to you."

Stephanie clicked off her phone and stared at George. "Clara's doing it again. She's gone to the fairgrounds to meet a murderer."

George rolled his eyes. "What?"

Stephanie repeated what Rick had told her. "Oh, George, why didn't she tell me where she was going? I could have stopped her—or at least done something to help her."

"You know Clara. No one can stop her once she's made up her mind about something."

"But why didn't she take me along? Why did she have to go by herself? Why did she have to go there at all?"

"All questions that will be answered when you hear from her. I'm sure—" He broke off as Stephanie's phone sang out again.

She slapped it to her ear. "Hello? Clara?"

"No, it's me again."

Stephanie gripped the phone harder and grabbed hold of George's hand. Rick's voice held a grim note that frightened her. "What's happened?"

"I don't know yet. I talked to Wes. He knows nothing about a meeting at the fairgrounds. I'm on my way there now. Wes is meeting me there. I'll call you as soon as I know anything."

Stephanie held back a groan. "Thank you, Rick. Please call me as soon as you can."

"I will." He hung up, and she flung her arms around George, tears coursing down her cheeks. "I knew it," she wailed. "Wes didn't know anything about a meeting. I knew she was in trouble. Why would she say she was meeting Wes if he knows nothing about it? I have to go there."

George's voice rose in alarm. "Go where?"

"To the fairgrounds. Maybe I can help." She pulled out of George's arms. "I have to go!"

"No, you don't." George gently but firmly pushed her down on the couch. "This time I'm not letting you go."

Stephanie looked up at her husband. His face looked blurred through her tears, and she blinked them away. "Maybe we should call the police."

George took the phone from her hand. "I'll have a word with Dan. If anything bad is going on, he'll want to know about it."

Stephanie watched anxiously as George talked to the dispatcher, then hung up. "What did he say?"

"Harry's going to relay the message to Dan, then it will be up to him what he does."

Stephanie sighed. "I guess we can't do anything else now but wait."

George sat down next to her and took her hand. "We'll wait together."

It was small comfort, but Stephanie was glad he was beside her. She had a feeling it was going to be a long night.

Changing direction, Clara sprinted for the fence. If she could just climb over it, she'd be safe. The pounding hooves were close behind her—so close she could hear the heavy panting of the bull. She reached the fence, got one foot on the bottom slat and grabbed the top one. Before she could haul herself over, Ferocious was on her.

By a miracle, his horn missed her, but as he thundered past he bumped her, brushing her off the fence as if she were a fly.

She sprawled in the sawdust, sending up a cloud of dust that burned her eyes and choked her throat. Coughing, she thought she heard a shout in the distance, but all her attention was on the bull.

Ferocious stood just a few feet away, his head lowered. His eyes mirrored the glow from a streetlamp and gleamed at her like devil eyes. She knew he was waiting for her to move. She also knew if she did so, the bull would be on her before she could climb the fence.

Her stomach heaved, and she closed her eyes, praying as she'd never prayed before.

As if in answer to her prayers, a quiet voice spoke out of the darkness. "Don't move a muscle."

Recognizing Wes's voice, she almost cried out. Biting back the sound, she froze, hardly daring to breathe.

At the sound of the voice, the bull had turned his head. He snorted, and pawed the ground with his forefoot.

Clara knew what that meant. He was getting ready to charge. She closed her eyes again.

In the next instant, all hell broke loose. Shouts, lights, the pounding of hooves, hollering and the sudden shock of being grabbed by two strong arms took all the breath from her body.

Dimly she was aware of being dragged over the fence, while the uproar inside the arena continued.

She was in Rick's arms, his hand cradling her head. "Are you hurt? Did he get you?"

Choking back tears, she shook her head. "Just a bruise or two. His horn missed me by inches."

"Thank God." Rick pulled her even closer. "If that beast had hurt you I would have killed it with my bare hands."

Clara thought that was pretty unlikely, but it was very satisfying to hear. "Thank heavens you got my message. I thought I was going to die."

"You can thank Stephanie. She was worried that you hadn't called her so she called me. That's when I found your message. We couldn't get you on your cell so I called Wes. He didn't know anything about meeting you here, so we came out to see what was going on." He shuddered. "That's when we saw Ferocious in the arena. We didn't see you until the bull starting charging at you." He tightened his arms around her. "When I saw him get that close to you on the fence and you fell . . ." He buried his face in her hair.

She hugged him, and after a moment he lifted his head. "Promise me you will never do anything like that again."

"Not if I can help it." Realizing the noise in the arena had subsided, she looked over the fence. Someone had switched on the arena lights. Wes was standing over by the chutes talking to a couple of guys. They must have been alerted by the noise. Behind them, a very unhappy bull stood corralled behind a gate.

"Wes saved my life," she said breathlessly. "I don't know how I'm going to thank him."

"Well, I like to think I had a hand in it, too. It wasn't easy going in there with that monster standing over you."

"Oh, I know." She looked up at him. "But I figured I'd thank you in a way I couldn't possibly manage with Wes."

Rick's eyes lit up. "Is that a promise?"

"You bet it is." She looked back at Wes. "You were right about him. He didn't kill Lisa."

"You sound very sure of that. Do you know who did?"

"I think so."

"So who was it?"

She was about to answer when another voice spoke from a few feet away. "That's something I'd like to know."

Swinging around, Clara looked into the disgruntled face of Dan Petersen. Tim hovered behind him, looking worried.

She looked back at Rick. "You called the police?"

"No," Dan said. "Your cousin's husband called me. He said you were in danger out here." He looked at Rick. "It doesn't look to me like you're in danger."

"Well, I was," Clara said, feeling guilty. Stephanie and George must have been really worried to call Dan. She quickly told the police chief everything that had happened to her that evening, emphasizing how Marty had tried to run her down on the coast road. "He killed Lisa Warren," she said when she was done. "I'm sure of it. He knew I was onto him and tried to kill me."

Dan shook his head. "Marty Pearce has a cast-iron alibi for that night. Just because the guy didn't see you in the dark doesn't make him a murderer. He could have been so shocked he froze on the brake. It's happened plenty of times before. I've done it myself." He stared across the arena at the men beside the chutes. "Is that Carlton over there?"

"He saved my life," Clara said quickly. "I would have been killed by that bull if Wes hadn't gotten here in time."

"He got the bull's attention and somehow got him in the chutes," Rick added. "He deserves a medal, if you ask me."

"He deserves more than that," Clara added fervently.

Dan stuck a hand in his pants pocket. "Didn't you tell me that he was the one who got you here in the first place? That he sent Marty Pearce to find you and bring you here?"

"But he didn't." She glanced up at Rick. "He didn't know anything about me coming here. That's why he and Rick came, to find out what was going on." She looked back at Dan. "Marty made all that up to get me out here. He left me alone in there with that bull, and if Wes and Rick hadn't turned up when they did, I wouldn't be standing here talking to you now."

Dan still looked unconvinced. "How do you know Carlton isn't lying about sending Pearce to find you?"

"Why would Wes risk his life to save me, if he wanted me dead?"

Dan pursed his lips. Before he could answer, Clara added, "What's more, I believe that Marty killed Seth Ferguson. It wasn't Marty in the arena that night Lisa was killed. He paid Seth to take his place. If you don't believe me, look at the video of that night on the *Chronicle*'s website. Sparky the clown is running around without a trace of a limp. Ask Marty to explain that."

Dan raised his eyebrows, while Rick murmured, "Nice work, detective."

Dan turned to Tim. "Find Marty Pearce and bring him to the station." He looked back at Clara. "We'll get all this sorted out tomorrow. Be in my office at nine a.m. sharp."

Clara let out her breath. "I'll be there."

"Meanwhile," Dan said, "I'll have a chat with Carlton." He started to walk off, then looked back at Clara over his shoulder. "If you're right about this, I'll take back everything I said about you interfering."

Clara smiled. "I can't wait."

———

"So are you going to tell us what happened at the police station, Clara?" Jessie demanded, as she handed a dish of roasted potatoes to Rick.

Clara piled some asparagus on her plate and passed the dish to her mother. "There's not a lot to tell."

Jessie sighed and shook her head at Rick. "She keeps

saying that. I was hoping she'd tell us more when you got here."

"I told you, Dan didn't tell me much. He was too busy asking me questions." Clara heaped potatoes on her plate.

"Actually, Wes told me some of it." Rick helped himself from the plate of salmon Jessie handed him. "He said Tim told him he found Marty soon after we left the arena. He was hooking up his trailer, getting ready to take off."

"Oh, my." Jessie offered Rick the wine bottle. "Good thing Tim caught up with him. He could have gone into hiding, and they never would have found him."

"Dan said Marty confessed to everything," Clara said, "once they showed him the video of the rodeo that night."

"I'm just surprised nobody else noticed that the clown wasn't limping." Jessie refilled her own glass with wine and passed the bottle to Clara.

"Marty did a good job of hiding his disability in the arena." Rick grinned at Clara. "But even he couldn't have done what Seth did that night without some sign of a limp. That was a great catch, Clara."

"It was, darling." Jessie smiled at her daughter. "I'm so proud of you. Did Marty say why he killed Lisa?"

"Dan didn't tell me anything except that Marty had confessed." Clara looked down at her plate. "He did congratulate me on figuring everything out."

"That's huge, coming from Dan." Rick raised his glass. "Here's to a job well done, detective!"

Jessie picked up her glass. "Good job, Clara, though I do wish you wouldn't take such awful risks. Especially when you're not getting paid to do it."

Clara laughed. "That's my mom. Practical as ever."

Jessie turned to Rick. "I don't suppose your friend knew why that dreadful man killed that poor woman?"

"As a matter of fact, he did. I guess Tim told him the whole story."

Clara uttered a little squeak of protest. "Why didn't you tell me?"

Rick grinned at her. "I haven't had the chance until now."

"So tell us!" Jessie leaned forward. "We're both panting to know."

"Apparently Marty was in love with Lisa. He made the mistake of telling her, and she laughed at him. I believe her actual words were something like, 'Why on earth would you think I'd be interested in a freak?'"

Clara gasped. "No wonder he was furious with her."

"Still," Jessie said, putting down her glass, "that didn't give him the right to kill her."

Clara stared at her plate, remembering the clown's words. *People think that because I'm a clown they can laugh at anything and everything I say or do. They don't think I have feelings just like everybody else.* "That's so sad. He lived to make people laugh, while inside he was miserable. That must have been so hard."

"It doesn't justify what he did," Jessie said firmly.

"He must have been burning up with revenge." Rick shook his head. "He'd heard the rumors about Lisa having an affair with Paul, so he forged a note from him to get Lisa to the concert stage. He said if he couldn't have her he'd make sure no one else would. So he strangled her."

Clara shuddered. "What about the pigging string? Where did he get that?"

"The what?" Jessie stared at her. "What on earth is that?"

"It's a rope the cowboys use to tie down calves." Clara looked at Rick. "Did he just happen to find it?"

"No, he stole it. He'd heard Wes fighting with Lisa about the way she'd treated him that afternoon, and he figured Wes would be blamed for the murder."

Jessie made a sound of disgust. "And what about Seth? Where did he figure in all this?"

Rick took a sip of his wine and put down the glass. "Marty knew Seth from his days on the circuit. He told Seth he'd been hired to work a benefit at a local hospital and that he wanted to do it but he'd be breaking his contract. So he offered to pay Seth to take his place. Seth couldn't resist getting back in the arena one more time."

"And it cost him his life," Clara said soberly.

Rick nodded. "Yeah, apparently Seth got suspicious when he heard about Lisa's death. He went down to the pub that night to question Marty, and got run down for his troubles. Tim found traces of Seth's blood on the fender of Marty's truck."

Jessie shivered. "How devious. He planned to murder that woman, and went to a lot of trouble to cover it up. Then he killed an innocent man to escape justice, and would have killed you, Clara, had this young man here not arrived in time to save you."

"Yes," Rick said, with a wicked wink at her. "You promised to thank me for that. Remember?"

Clara felt her cheeks warm as she caught her mother's interested glance. "I have to thank Stephanie, too," she said quickly. "If she hadn't called you, you might never have seen that message on your phone until it was too late."

"True." Rick picked up his fork. "Your cousin said she had a feeling you were in danger. You two must be really close to tune in to each other like that. Though you do seem to have a knack for reading people's minds."

Clara froze. Had her mother told him about the Sense after all? She looked at Jessie and met her mother's steady gaze.

Jessie gave an imperceptible shake of her head. "Clara has always been sensitive to people's moods," she said lightly.

Clara relaxed. She should have known her mother would keep quiet about something her daughter so desperately wanted to keep hidden. She felt reasonably secure in the knowledge that the Quinn Sense would remain a family secret—at least for now.

Smiling, she raised a glass. "Let's drink a toast. To family and friends."

Rick raised his glass, his gaze warm on her face. "To friendship and love."

"I'll drink to that," Jessie murmured.

Clara barely noticed. She was too busy staring into Rick's eyes.

Turn the page for an excerpt
from the second
Raven's Nest Bookstore mystery

A Sinister Sense

available now in paperback
from Berkley Prime Crime

1

Clara Quinn was in the act of rearranging a display of cookbooks when she heard the ruckus. It sounded like a big dog in a tizzy. A *really* big dog. After trying for several moments to ignore the commotion, she walked over to the bookstore's window to get a better look.

Outside, the afternoon heat shimmered on the cars passing by, dazzling her eyes. A group of summer visitors wandered along the storefronts, seeking the shade of the striped awnings as they hunted for souvenirs. Some of them paused to watch the cause of the disturbance—a shaggy black and gray dog leaping up and down, barking at a tall, blonde woman.

Clara winced. Roberta Prince, owner of the stationer's next door, would not appreciate being pawed by a dog.

Roberta never appeared in public without perfect makeup, an impeccable hairdo and an immaculate outfit.

One muddy paw print on that slim, white skirt or, worse, the coral silk shirt, and the image would be destroyed. Roberta's day would be ruined, and everyone else around her would feel the repercussions.

As Clara watched, the irate woman backed off into the road. The dog advanced, apparently determined to knock her down. Roberta must have lost her nerve. She turned tail and dashed across to the nearest haven, which just happened to be the Raven's Nest bookstore.

Unfortunately the door was on a strong spring. It didn't close quite fast enough as Roberta charged through it, followed closely by her pursuer.

Roberta yelped and rushed toward the counter. The dog chased after her, its tail thrashing wildly. Colliding with the table, it sent Clara's intricate display of cookbooks tumbling to the floor.

"Hey!" Clara flew over to the animal and grabbed its collar before it could do any more damage. The dog lunged forward, dragging her with it.

"Tatters! *Sit!*"

The loud bellow had come from the open doorway. In all the uproar, Clara hadn't noticed Rick Sanders blocking out the sunlight. Rick owned the hardware store across the street and, by the looks of it, a very unruly animal.

Clara let go of the collar, allowing the big dog to trot around the counter, once more in pursuit of Roberta.

"Get that thing *away* from me!" Roberta flapped her hand at the dog, making it bark once more.

"Tatters!" Rick slammed the door shut behind him and strode forward, one hand raised in the air. "Here, boy. *Now!*"

Tatters ignored him and went on barking—loud, deep barks that seemed to reverberate throughout the shop.

Clara moved around the counter, leaned forward and laid a hand on the back of the dog's neck. "It's all right, Tatters. Just calm down, baby."

Tatters whined and turned his head to look at her.

Cautiously, Roberta moved around the end of the counter. "You need to control that monster," she hissed at Rick as she hurried to the door and hauled it open. "It's a menace."

Rick looked hurt. "He's just a dog. He thought you had more cookies, that's all."

Roberta brushed imaginary hairs from her skirt and sent a disdainful glare at the offending animal. "That's not a dog. It's a . . . big . . . hairy . . . *horse*." With that, she swept out of the shop and disappeared up the street.

Clara met Rick's gaze and burst out laughing. "I guess she's not a dog lover."

Rick's expression was grim. "I can't really blame her. Look at him. He takes up more room than my truck. The thing *is* a menace."

Clara patted the silky coat and received a moist lick on her hand in gratitude. "Oh, he's not yours, then?"

"Not if I can help it." Still scowling, Rick joined her

behind the counter, where Tatters now sat panting, his tongue flopping out of his mouth.

Snapping the leash he held onto the dog's collar, Rick glanced up at her. "You seem to have a way with dogs."

The comment made Clara uncomfortable. She'd spent most of her life hiding the fact that the infamous sixth sense she'd inherited from her family gave her special insights into people's minds. Not only people, it seemed, but animals as well. At least to the point where she could communicate with them in a way they understood. Some of the time, anyway.

The family called it the Quinn Sense. Not everyone inherited it, much to the disgust of Clara's cousin, Stephanie, who owned the Raven's Nest, loved all things paranormal and never got over the fact that the family curse, as Clara called it, had bypassed her.

Born just two months apart and more like sisters than cousins, she and Stephanie had grown up together, planned futures together, dreamed dreams together. They'd eagerly awaited the day when their powers would be fully developed. When they'd realized that Clara had the Quinn Sense and her cousin did not, it had caused an uneasy rift between the two of them. Unspoken, but there all the same.

"Did I say something wrong?"

Clara jumped, realizing that Rick was staring at her, no doubt confused with her silence. "I'm sorry, I was just thinking about Roberta and wondering why Tatters chased her across the street."

Rick made a sound of disgust in his throat. "She came into the store with a handful of cookies for the dog. I don't know how she knew he was there. That woman doesn't miss anything that goes on in Main Street. Or the whole of Finn's Harbor, come to that."

Clara grinned. "She does have an ear for gossip. People are calling her Maine's main mole."

A smile flicked across his face. "Cute. I like it."

"She doesn't."

"Yeah, I can imagine."

"So she gave Tatters the cookies?"

Rick nodded. "I warned her not to, but of course she didn't listen. The dog wasn't happy with what she gave him, so he started sniffing around her, looking for more. She backed off and he took it as a game. Before I could stop him, he'd chased her out of the store and across the street."

Clara couldn't resist another grin. "Yeah, I saw her."

"I had a customer back there thinking about buying a very expensive lawn mower. There's another guy asking where to find City Hall and someone else looking at garden tools. They've probably gone by now. Thanks to this brute."

Clara leaned down to pat the dog's head. "Oh, poor Tatters. You just wanted to play, didn't you?" She looked up at Rick. "Tatters?"

Rick pulled a face at her as he led the dog over to the door. "My ex-wife called him Tatters because he looked a mess when we rescued him from the pound. Lisa fought tooth and nail to keep him after the divorce, and now, all of a sudden, she wants to dump him on me." He hauled open the door, and Tatters made a leap for freedom, dragging Rick hard against the doorjamb.

He grunted with pain, and Clara screwed up her face in sympathy. Rick, it seemed, was not having a good day, what with the disobedient dog and the bandage she'd just noticed adorning the forefinger of his right hand.

Bracing his foot against the wall, Rick hauled on the leash. "She's got a new boyfriend who hates dogs. To be more specific, he hates Tatters. So now I'm supposed to give him a home? What the heck does she think I'm going to do with him? I can't leave him alone in the house. He'll wreck the place the minute I'm gone."

Clara wasn't quite sure how to respond to that. She'd known Rick just a few months, and they'd become friendly enough to talk about a few things on a personal level. This was the first time, however, that Rick had mentioned his ex-wife.

Of course, there were a lot of things she hadn't told him, either, but somehow an ex-wife seemed a very significant part of his past, and the fact he hadn't once spoken of her suggested a pretty bad split between them.

"I'm sure you'll be able to work things out," she said, mostly because Rick was looking at her as if he expected her to solve his problem. "He seems like a sweet dog and just needs a little attention, that's all."

"He needs a lot more than attention. He needs discipline. Look at him. He's just waiting for the chance to break free again." He waved a hand at Tatters, who now stood looking at him, tail wagging, waiting for his master's next move.

Rick's gray eyes were full of desperation when he looked back at her. "I don't suppose you know anyone who could tame this tiger?"

She hesitated, eager to help but unsure what it would entail. She liked Rick. Really liked him. If things had been different, if she'd never met the man of her dreams in New York, only to find out he was a cheat and a liar, she might have encouraged Rick to take their relationship further.

The pain of her breakup, however, was still fresh in her mind. Even though it had been almost a year since she'd moved back to Finn's Harbor, she was far from ready to trust her heart to anyone yet. No one, she'd vowed, was ever going to hurt her that badly again.

As far as Rick was concerned, she'd managed to keep things uncomplicated, and he seemed to be comfortable with that arrangement. She enjoyed his friendship and was careful not to get into situations that could jeopardize that by letting something more personal creep in.

She was still trying to figure out how she could work with the dog without spending too much time with his owner when Rick said quietly, "It's okay. Forget I mentioned it. Maybe I'll just try to find a home for him. Somewhere where he can run about without demolishing everything that he comes in contact with."

He gave her a quick wave before being dragged across the street by the enthusiastic Tatters.

Watching them go, Clara suddenly noticed a tingling awareness washing over her. She knew the sensation well. She was about to hear voices in her head—voices that spoke in riddles and phrases she couldn't understand. Voices that led her down paths she didn't want to go, and put obstacles in her way to prevent her from following her instincts.

Her reaction was automatic and swift. Closing off her mind, she hurried down to the Reading Nook, where a comfortable couch and a pot of coffee awaited her.

Ever since she'd realized that she had the Quinn Sense and Stephanie didn't, she'd felt isolated somehow. Although most of the family had some degree of psychic ability, she'd kept hers a secret. Far from being the empowering, exciting and liberating experience the cousins had imagined, being able to interpret dreams and occasionally read minds and foretell the future had made Clara feel like a freak.

Desperate to regain some sense of normalcy, she'd left Maine to attend college in New York, where no one knew her or her family. She'd soon discovered that, hard as she tried, she couldn't escape the infamous legacy. The Quinn Sense continued to interfere with her life and mess up her mind.

Worse, it was unpredictable—never there when she needed it, and intruding when she least expected it. When the Sense had failed to prevent her from making the biggest mistake of her life, the betrayal was the last straw. On her thirtieth birthday she'd picked up the pieces and come home to Finn's Harbor.

Her cell phone sang out just then, shattering her

thoughts. Stephanie's voice buzzed in her ear, full of tension and anxiety as usual.

"Clara! I just read in the *Chronicle* that the sales of e-books are taking over print versions. What are we going to do? I *knew* I shouldn't have leased that store. What was I thinking? This is the absolute *worst* time to own a bookstore!"

Clara sighed. She'd had this conversation with her cousin more than once, and each time Stephanie had been certain she was headed for bankruptcy. "Calm down, Steffie. The world isn't going to end just because a few misinformed fanatics go around waving placards saying it is. Books are going to be around for at least as long as you'll want to sell them."

"Yes, but if everyone is reading them on electronic readers, who's going to buy print books?"

"Everyone who doesn't like electronic readers. More than enough people to keep you in business for a long time, I promise you."

Stephanie's sigh echoed down the line. "I hope you're right. George keeps telling me the same thing, but then husbands always tell their wives what they want to hear. I just can't help feeling I should have opened a knitting shop instead."

Clara rolled her eyes. "You've never knitted anything in your life."

"What difference does that make?"

"You've spent your entire life immersed in magic and all things paranormal. With all the interest in it now, opening a bookstore specializing in the occult was a brilliant idea, and you are the perfect person to do it, so stop obsessing over things you can't control. The Raven's Nest is doing just fine. Especially since you opened the Reading Nook. Half the town comes here for the coffee and donuts."

"I know you're right." Stephanie paused, then added in a rush, "I just wish I had the Sense, like you. It would have made planning things so much easier."

Deciding this was the perfect time to change the subject, Clara launched into a detailed account of Roberta's confrontation with Rick's dog.

Stephanie laughed through most of it, until Clara mentioned that Rick was thinking of finding the dog a home. "Oh, you can't let him do that!" Now her cousin sounded close to tears. "That poor dog has already lost one home. Think how awful it would be for him to go to strangers. Can't you look after him?"

"Me? Why me? I'm a stranger, too."

"Yes, but you have . . . you know . . ." Stephanie paused, obviously mindful of her cousin's adverse reaction whenever the Quinn Sense was mentioned.

"Just because I get along with dogs doesn't mean I want to adopt one," Clara said firmly. "Besides, can you imagine what my mother would say if I brought a dog that size into the house? She'd have hysterics."

"Well, you keep saying you're tired of living with Aunt Jessie and you want to find an apartment."

"I do, but so far my hunting for one has produced zero opportunities. Besides, an apartment manager is even less likely to view Tatters with a fond eye."

Stephanie giggled. "Tatters. What a ridiculous name."

Clara smiled. "Oddly enough, the name suits him."

"Oh, he sounds adorable. What a shame Rick can't keep him. I feel so bad for him. I wish—" She broke off, raising her voice to yell at an unseen child. "Michael? *Michael!* What are you doing with that tennis racket? *What?* No! You may *not* use it as a sled. Stay away from the stairs. You hear me?"

Clara held the phone away from her ear, well used to her cousin's tirades. Stephanie had three kids, and while Ethan, the eldest, lived in front of his computer and was barely seen or heard, Olivia and Michael spent most of their time seeing who could get into the most trouble.

"Sorry," Stephanie muttered, when apparently peace was restored. "What was I saying? Oh, yes, about the dog. Surely there's some way Rick could keep him? Can't you talk to him? Persuade him to give Tatters a second chance?"

It was time to end the conversation, Clara decided. Her cousin was making her feel guilty, which was ridiculous, of course. She had no good reason to feel guilt over what was Rick's problem and Rick's alone.

After she hung up, she poured herself a cup of coffee and tried to relax, but the uncomfortable feeling still gnawed away at her stomach. She kept seeing the dog's dark brown eyes staring hopefully into hers, his tail slowly swishing back and forth.

There was nothing she could do, she reminded herself. Working full-time in the bookstore and living with her mom were two very good reasons she couldn't devote her time to training a lovable but totally undisciplined dog. Especially one that was almost as tall as her when standing on his hind legs—no mean feat, since she was five feet ten without her shoes.

Nope, Rick would just have to take care of his own problem. She just hoped he'd decide to keep the dog, so she wouldn't have to feel guilty anymore.

That night she dreamed a monster dog was chasing her along the beach. Her feet kept sinking in the sand, and the dog was drawing closer as she fought to outrun him. Then, without warning, he vanished.

She turned and saw him struggling in the ocean, being taken out to sea by massive waves. Horrified, she tried to jump into the water, only to be thrown back by the current. She woke up with a start, her heart beating rapidly, as if she'd actually been running.

Annoyed with herself, she threw the tangled covers aside and leapt out of bed. She was beginning to wish she'd never set eyes on Tatters. It was easy enough to interpret her dream. She was still racked with guilt for what felt like her abandonment of the animal.

She'd thought that her years in New York had toughened her up, but here she was, obsessing over a dog she'd known for all of ten minutes.

———

The feeling of anxiety that had bothered her ever since she'd fallen out of bed that morning was now a full-blown feeling of impending disaster. Hoping it wasn't the Quinn Sense giving her a warning, she shoved open the door and stepped inside the cool, shadowed entrance of the Raven's Nest.

As Clara walked over to the counter, Stephanie called out to her. Balanced on the rung of a ladder and half-hidden behind a stack of books, she peered out from one of the aisles. "Have you heard the news?"

Clara paused. The sensation was back. She could hear them now—the voices, clamoring in her head. She struggled to banish them. "What news?"

A face popped up from behind the counter, crowned with flyaway red hair. Molly Owens's bright blue eyes sparkled with excitement. "We've been waiting for you to get here. You won't believe what's happened. There's been a murder!"

The voices were immediately silenced, leaving only a cold sick feeling behind. Clara's lips felt dry as she answered Molly. "Where? Here in Finn's Harbor?"

Stephanie abandoned her books and hurried over to join her young assistant behind the counter. "We thought you might have heard it on the news."

Clara shook her head. "I was listening to a CD in my car. Who died? Not anyone we know, I hope."

Molly was practically jumping up and down. "No one knows who he is. The police found him this morning. Guess where!"

You don't want to know. Clara jumped. It was as if someone had spoken the words out loud in her ear. She looked at Stephanie for help.

Her cousin's face was a picture of discomfort. "I'm sorry, Clara. I know you like him, but . . ." She hesitated, and before Clara could absorb the words, Molly jumped in to finish for her.

"They found the body in the back of Rick Sanders's truck!"